T0196127

# Ancestral Meridians

Odie Hawkins

authorHOUSE®

AuthorHouse™
1663 Liberty Drive
Bloomington, IN 47403
www.authorhouse.com
Phone: 1 (800) 839-8640

Front Cover by Sunhee Hong
Sunheedesign.wordpress.com
http://www.cafepress.com/sunheedesign

Author's Photo by Zola Salena-Hawkins
www.flickr.com/photos/32886903@N02

Published by AuthorHouse    02/16/2017

ISBN: 978-1-5246-7249-2 (sc)
ISBN: 978-1-5246-7247-8 (hc)
ISBN: 978-1-5246-7248-5 (e)

Library of Congress Control Number: 2017902531

Print information available on the last page.

Any people depicted in stock imagery provided by Thinkstock are models,
and such images are being used for illustrative purposes only.
Certain stock imagery © Thinkstock.

This book is printed on acid-free paper.

Because of the dynamic nature of the Internet, any web addresses or links contained in
this book may have changed since publication and may no longer be valid. The views
expressed in this work are solely those of the author and do not necessarily reflect the
views of the publisher, and the publisher hereby disclaims any responsibility for them.

*Dedicated to Dr. Jewel Thais-Williams, Dr. Daniel Hoover, Mrs. Veronika Hoover, Dr. Jonathan Lin, Dr. Coco Chin and to our friend, Master Tam Tran, for his patient and expert teaching of Tai Chi, the Dao, the Cane and the Fan.*

## ANCESTRAL MERIDIANS

*"A ninth planet has been discovered. All of the details have not been revealed about how much is known, or unknown about this planet, other than the fact that it is ten times larger than Earth. It has been tentatively named #9 and that's it for the moment. Stay tuned."*

# Contents

# CHAPTER 1

DR. JONATHAN HOOVER SETTLED BACK in his upholstered desk chair, slowly unwrapped his Carpal tunnel preventive glove from his right hand and stared at the paragraph he had just written.

Wonder where that came from? He smiled. No questions, Doc, just go with the flow. Just go with the flow. His smile was replaced by a serious frown. He was finding it harder and harder to, *"Just go with the flow."* Seems that it would be easy to simply sit here and scribble about the things that've happened in my life over the course of my past fifty odd years as a practitioner, a Doctor of Holistic Medicine.

"Jonathan, I think you should write your autobiography. I can't think of anyone who has had a more interesting life. After all, let's face it, you probably won't live another seventy-five years . . . ."

Well, I guess that's the sort of thing the woman you've been married to for the past fifty years would say. "Jonathan, I think you should write your autobiography." It took him a couple years to take her frequently offered advice – "Jonathan, I think . . . ."

The frown surrendered to another smile. If there was one thing he loved and admired about Verona Obregon-Hoover, it was her persistence.

If she felt strongly about something, she would stick with it 'til the end.

"Jonathan, can I make a suggestion?"

"Be my guest."

"I think ...."

"I know, you think I ought to write my autobiography?"

"That doesn't sound like a bad idea. What do you think?"

She cornered him with her persistence, hugs and gentle kisses on his eyes, cheeks and lips, his weak spots. A week after he had taken the advice she had been giving him for two solid years, he was working his way through his first draft outline.

Always have to have a foundation, the road map needed to tell you where to start, what to do in the middle, and how to end it. Whatever it was. He had discovered that it was much easier spoken about than done after the first day of working on an outline for "Ancestral Meridians."

It became "Ancestral Meridians" after he did a mental review of the story one of his patients had revealed to him. Easier talked about than written about. He had spent the better part of his first writing afternoon drinking Jasmine tea and staring at the blank pages on his desk.

By the end of the afternoon, he hadn't smothered the pages in front of him with words, but he had made a stab at a beginning – "Jonathan Hoover, seventy-five years old, "retired." Fifty solid years of Holistic Medicine, learning and using his skills as a chiropractor, an herbalist, an acupuncturist, a martial artist." "Retired?"

"Dr. Hoover, we are pleased and honored to present this award to you, for your distinguished service in the arts of healing."

He did a slow, careful pan of the awarded plaques, on his office wall, the weird statutes, the scrolls he had received as trophy rewards for his "distinguished, brilliant career."

"Thank you, thank all of you."

## XXX    XXX

Two days later, he had found a way into his story. Write a long letter to yourself, his subconscious said to him, one that would be of interest to more people other than Verona Obregon-Hoover.

"Jonathan, I don't think you have to be too concerned about whether or not there's an audience for your story, I think you should just write it . . . ."

Go with the flow, Doc, go with the flow.

## XXX    XXX

"I was one of the chosen people, that's how one of my friends described us, one of the two hundred and twelve students given the privilege of attending the Society of Healing Martial Arts Academy (SoHMAA.) Expensive, but lenient with scholarship stuff.

Dr. Anouska Mehta was the leading light of SoHMAA.

"The name might be a bit misleading for some people, so please allow me to make it perfectly clear what we are doing here. Fifty years ago, a collection, maybe they could be called a coalition of Chinese and American doctors decided to share their knowledge of medicine. Quite a radical idea for the times, when you think about it.

I don't need to give you a grocery list of their names; you can find them on the large stone plaque above the entrance on the first floor. As I was about to say, allow me to make it perfectly clear what we are doing here.

We are a "society," within the commonly understood use of that term, but we are not the elitist folks that some have attached to our use of the word. I hope you are following me.

"Healing Martial Arts." Nowadays, when many people think of the martial arts as destructive engines, it's difficult for them to conceive of the martial arts as anything but hurt 'em, kill 'em stuff. That's not where I'm at, that's not where SoHMAA is.

Yes, of course, most of our staff are martial artists in one style or another. No problem. We feel that the practice of a martial art is entirely consistent with our stated goal, which is to try to combat physical and mental challenges human beings face with the right application of the right medicine. Some of the medicine might involve physical and mental self-defense techniques.

Dr. Mehta, a crusty case with a critically sweet heart.

"Mr. Hoover, you have to understand this simple fact – SoHMAA exists to give our patients the best treatment, the best care they could possibly have. We have a very high bar and attached to that bar is the sign – 'Superior served here.' Are you getting me, Mr. Hoover?"

"Loud'n clear, Dr. Mehta, loud'n clear."

## XXX    XXX

"I can't begin to tell you how it happened, or when I first had the experience of feeling/knowing that I could take the limbs of the human body into my hands, literally, and straighten them out. Of course, it took many years of serious study for me to clearly understand what my Abuela Ana had taught me, years before I enrolled in SoHMAA.

I didn't know that my grandmother (father's mother) was a cuarandera until I had spent my first year at SoHMAA. I still find it hard to explain what a cuarandera is. Whenever I go back to Huatabampo, our ancestral home in Mexico, the meaning of the word seems to have changed a bit, depending on what has happened concerning a cuarandera or a cuarandero.

If, for example, a cuarandera has been involved with saving somebody's life, or doing some other good thing, by using her knowledge of herbs, then she will be highly thought of, praised as a savior. But if something bad has happened – let's say, she has tried to use her expertise to help a family get rid of bad luck, malditos, and her stuff doesn't work, then she might be thought to be a witch.

My Abuela Ana was <u>never</u> accused of being a bruja, a witch, thank God. And I'm very pleased to say that she was a great prep school for SoHMAA. I felt at ease with the herbal remedies, with the acupuncture, but I really found my sweet spot in chiropractic work.

Like I said earlier, I can't begin to tell you how it happened, or when I first had the experience of feeling/knowing that I could take the limbs of a human body in my hands, literally, and straighten them out. I'm proud to say Abuela Ana was present at my graduation from SoHMAA, when I was privileged to call myself Doctor Jonathan Hoover.

Later, on her death bed, at the age of one hundred and four, she shared many of her secrets about healing. I have no doubts that a lot of what she shared with me has made me a better doctor, better than any degree could identify or signify.

O, about the name … Hoover. Remember we've had Mexicans named O'Brian, Kahlo, Haro, Slivowitsh, and Fox. Mexico is a very diverse society."

XXX       XXX

"I'm proud to be a Native American, a Lakota Sioux, to be exact, and the head of the herbal section of SoHMAA. It would take a lot of hours to explain how Sam Young Hawk, one of the great-great-great- grandsons of Chief Sitting Bull, became a member of an institution that focused on

4

some of the same healing practices that my ancestors practiced, natural herbs for natural healing, for a natural life.

I had doubts about becoming a student at SoHMAA. Why shouldn't I have doubts? If there is one thing that Native people have grown to understand, since the invasion/conquering of our land, by the Europeans, we must <u>not</u> trust them because they are liars and thieves.

Liars and thieves. I had all that stuff in mind when I was offered a scholarship to SoHMAA. I talked to my grandfather back on the Rosebud Res – Medicine Man Buffalo Wovoka.

'Grandfather, they want me to be the headman of the herbal section ...'

'Sam, does that mean that they are going to honor any of the treaties that they never honored? Does that mean that they are going to <u>try</u> to clean up this mess that they've made of this land? With all of their pollution and stupid greed. Does that mean that you will become the Chief of something with no power?'

I had to think on that one for a bit. As the head of the herbal section at SoHMAA, I would have control of how people became aware of the power of herbs for the process of healing.

'Oh, one more thing, Sam, just make sure they don't pay you with no wooden nickels ... hahhahhah... or give you any contaminated blankets.'

Grandfather Buffalo Wovoka was always joking (?) with me about my relationships with White people. To be honest about it, there were times when I didn't know if he was joking or not. Just a few more words about my grandfather.

He was the son (on his paternal side) of my great-grandfather, Bear Brother, who was one of the last Native Americans who had done the Ghost Dance back in 1870. The Ghost Dance movement was started by the great Paiute Shaman, Wovoka. Wovoka, in his Dream, had gone up to Heaven for a meeting with God. He said that God told him to return and tell the People that they must be good and love one another, and not fight, or steal, or lie. He said that God gave him the Ghost Dance. The Ghost Dance was going to cause the White people to be swallowed up by the Earth and living and dead Indians would be reunited. He offered <u>resurrection</u> for the Native Americans. Needless to say, the Ghost Dance caused a lot of heat to come down on those who were involved in it, and many who were <u>not</u> involved.

In any case, my great grandfather had been a Ghost Dancer before he was killed by White settlers in South Dakota. He named my grandfather Buffalo Wovoka to honor the memory of the prophet Wovoka.

I spent a lot of time thinking about Wovoka, my great grandfather, my father and mother, and all of those heroic men and women who had fought so hard to maintain their cultures, their way of life. I went up into the Sequoia forest in Northern California for a seven-day fast. I wanted to make certain that I was going to do honor to my heritage by accepting a very responsible position.

Seems that I did the right thing because there are times when I feel that the herbs are speaking to me, in my great grandfather's voice."

XXX     XXX

"Jonathan, dinner is ready, you feel like taking a little break?"

"Verona, are you kidding me? I can't think of anything I need to write that would stop me from having one of your fried pompano dinners."

He unwound the Carpal tunnel syndrome glove from his right hand, marked his stopping point with a ledger of ebony wood. They strolled through the long polished hallway leading to the dining room.

What a blessing this woman is to me, has been to me. He gave her a gentle peck on the cheek. She returned the cheek peck with a slight squeeze of his waist. Whole pompano fish, salted/peppered/dill spiced, battered in corn meal, steamed rice, stir fried okra with cumin, fresh small onions and sliced tomatoes with a few sprinkles of cilantro on top. One of his favorite dinners.

Verona served him. The fish was sliced in half. He liked to eat the rear half first, a few tablespoons of rice on one side of the plate, the okra and salad on the other side. A beautiful composition.

"What would you like to drink?"

"I would like to lie and say that I want a glass of juice, but I'd prefer a glass of the Vouray. It would go perfect with this."

"You got it. I just happened to have a bottle chilling in the fridge. Be right back."

She knows me like a well-read book. What could go better than a glass of good French wine with a dinner like this? The wine poured, a few bites into the deliciously textured fish....

"So, how's it going?"

"I'm glad you asked; I've been dying to talk to somebody about the direction this thing seems to be going." Talk to "somebody?" she smiled. They were always "playing with each other.

"Sounds like you're talking about something that's beginning to have a life of its own."

They did a ritualistic touching of wine glasses across the table.

"I really think that's what's beginning to happen. I learned, a long time ago, to go with the flow. Can't recall who first put that bug in my ear, but it's some of the best advice I've ever received. I was really worried for a minute, as you know, about how to get into this thing."

Dinner finished, they strolled out into their backyard, a half-acre of flowers, medicinal herbs, and wild life. It was one of their favorite at home things to do.

"Jonathan, you talk about going with the flow. What is the flow doing for you, what is it bringing to you?"

"Hmmmm, hard to say off hand. One of the things that's happening is that I'm revisiting a whole bunch of classmates."

"Have you spoken to Daniel about your project?"

"Not yet, not yet."

"You think he's going to be surprised to hear that you're writing your autobiography?"

"Probably not. You know how Daniel is; he's seldom surprised by anything. And besides, CoCo bugged him into start writing his story six months before you <u>forced</u> me into a writing mode. Now that I think about it – tell me, did you two, you and CoCo get some kind of bet on, as to which one of you could coerce your reluctant husband to write his story first?"

He loved the shy doe expression she used whenever she wanted to soften the edge of his question, or just charm him away from his point.

"You think that I and CoCo would have some sort of competition to provoke our husbands into writing their autobiography? You really think that, Jonathan?"

The shy expression slid into a kind of kitten-expression-of- innocence. Jonathan shook his head and was forced to smile at her game.

"Yes, Verona, I <u>do</u> think that." He felt he had managed her shy doe-kitten innocent expression bravely enough to give her a hard answer.

She curled up under his left armpit as they strolled back thru their garden into the house. One of her favorite "seduction positions."

"Well, am I right or wrong?" He pressed the question as they finished off the Vouray. She sipped, savoring the wine's flavors.

"Jonathan, let me put it to you this way. You and Daniel knew each other before me and CoCo met; me, your future wife and CoCo, Daniel's future wife. You guys bonded, and the same thing happened with me and CoCo.

Now, whether or not we competed to see which one of us could entice, coerce, seduce our 'retired' husbands into writing their incredibly interesting autobiographies – I can't say we did that or that we didn't do that."

"What's that mean?" They were both on the cusp of laughing.

"Depends on how you think about it. All I'm saying is that Daniel started writing his story about six months before you started yours …."

The shy doe expression shifted to a completely different expression, a foxy look. It was on, whatever it was.

## XXXX    XXX

"Awwww c'mon, Nelson, you know where all these points are – how 'bout giving me a little push here? The exam is three days away and I'm beginning to blank out. A little help, please. Please help SoHMAA buddy out . . ."

O God, here we go again; I'm the Chinese American guy that they assume to be an expert acupuncturist. How many different ways, how many times can I tell them that I'm working just as hard as everybody else to get this stuff right.

Why don't they go to Jonathan and Daniel? They seem to have a lock on this stuff. Acupuncture, of all things. Even Dr. Mehta thinks that I have a leg up on the acupuncture points and all the rest.

"So, Nelson, I don't think you'll find this particular section of our curriculum a serious problem."

Go 'head and say it, Doc. "Nelson Wang, you're Chinese, so this section shouldn't be problematic for you."

What a weird pressure point, or pressure points. I was pressuring myself because, I may as well confess, I felt that I was supposed to do well in acupuncture. After all, at the end of the day, I <u>am</u> Chinese and we did invent this way of dealing with pain.

"O.k. Jeff, relax, I'm gonna show you where the principal points are – are you ready?"

"Yes yes yes, thanks Nelson, thanks . . ."

Well, what could I do? I felt that I was damned if I did and damned if I didn't.

XXX  XXX

# CHAPTER 2

"CoCo, are you sitting down in there?"

"Do you want me to?"

Dr. Daniel Lane II rolled his eyes to the ceiling and smiled. That's right, CoCo, play games with me, I deserve it.

"Well, not really. It's just that I thought you would like to be seated when I gave you the news . . ."

CoCo Chen-Lane leaned against the doorway of her husband's library-study-workshop, long cooking chopsticks in hand.

"What news? Give it to me quick or else I'll burn the egg rolls."

"Mmmmm, so that's what I've been smelling . . ."

"Quick, the news?"

"You asked me yesterday, when've you talked to Jonathan? I told you it's been a couple weeks. . ."

"Very unusual for you guys – what's the news?"

"He just tested me, he's writing his autobiography."

"Really? That is news . . . oopps – gotta tend to the egg rolls."

He turned back to the outline he was using for his autobiography – "In the Slow Lane" by Daniel Lane II.

She didn't seem to be as surprised as I thought she would be. O well.

The chef flicked two crisply browned egg rolls into a bamboo basket lined with absorbent tissue. So, Verona has finally stirred Jonathan into writing his book. This ought to be an interesting summer. A big smile slid across her face.

XXX     XXX

"I think I must be very careful how I say this, but I must be honest. I think it becomes much easier to tell the truth about things that have happened, when you are older. I'm eighty-five years old now, not eighty-five years young, as this youth oriented society wants to portray us. I think there is something fraudulent about that, about wanting to portray older people as 'young' because they fear becoming old.

They fear becoming old, so they label us, the active old people, as young. It's a buffer zone for them, I think, to portray active older people as young. It means that they will never face the experience of becoming old. I stress the idea of active older people being considered 'young,' because that seems to animate the discussion. It shouldn't. The conversation about who can generate the most imaginative ideas should be the catalyst behind the conversations, not a title called 'age.'

Now, let me step off the soap box and talk a bit about two of the most brilliant and imaginative students I had during my twenty-five years as the Director of SoHMAA. I have to confess, at this late date, that I have retained a bit of bias concerning these two.

Number one, I immediately recognized that Jonathan Hoover and Daniel Lane II were exceptional individuals . . . from the first month they enrolled at SoHMAA. It was an intuitive thing, but I grew to accept my intuition, as an element of my analytic process many years ago.

I'm only ten years older than these two, but I'm sure that they saw me as an old, crusty, hard bitten academician, or something worse, when they first got to know me. I must confess, as the first Director of SoHMAA, and as an immigrant from Benares, India, I felt compelled to set the bar high.

I had no intention of having the State Board, or anyone else, come through SoHMAA and find anything substandard. I set the bar at Superior and challenged all of the students in our program to aim for that. Excellence would be, well, o.k., but superior was to be considered the norm. Jonathan and Daniel were ideal candidates for our program. And not simply because they were smart. They demonstrated four of the basic qualities that we felt to be the foundation for SoHMAA's success; integrity, morality, honor and a passion for helping humanity solve some of its health problems.

It didn't take me very long to determine that there was a bit of competitive edge between these two. It wasn't anything obnoxious or full blown, but it was there and I must confess that I made every effort to exploit this competitive edge. I felt it would be good for the student body to see that two of our best felt that they could be better, do better.

As a teacher I can honestly say it is quite rewarding to have had students like Jonathan Hoover and Daniel Lane II. It makes me feel as though all of my efforts to promote SoHMAA's program were not in vain . . . ."

XXX    XXX

The sign says – "Dr. Nzingha Howard" and I can tell you, straight up, I had a bunch of sorority sisters nag on me about getting into SoHMAA, into Holistic Medicine, about becoming a Doctor of Holistic Medicine.

"Awww c'mon, Nzingha, herbs are great to smoke and we all know about exercise and keeping your weight down by not eating too much, but the needles and all of this other stuff – gimme a break."

My Alpha sisters could talk to me like that because they had earned that right. We were there for each other. Kenya's comments were just one facet of the opinions offered about my choice of a career.

There were others, much more sympatica.

"Nzingha, looks like you're really gotten yourself into something. The only thing I can say to you is, from what I hear, is that you won't be making an awful lot of money, unless you become a female, African-American Deepock Chopra, or something like that."

"Filisteena, this is not about money."

"'Scuse me. . . .'"

"This is not about money . . ."

"But that's one of the big reasons why people go into medicine, to make the big bucks. Or marry a rich doctor."

"Filisteena, you are absolutely terrible!"

"You mean you're not interested in marrying a rich doctor?"

"The person I marry doesn't have to be a doctor or rich. I am not looking for one or the other. When I marry it's going to be for love."

"Love, huh? Well, I guess that's as good a reason as any to get married."

"Filisteena, we'll have to talk about all of this at another time, I'm expecting a patient in five minutes."

"Awright, girlfriend, we'll get together one day next week?"

"Call me. Gotta go, 'bye."

"'Bye."

Most of the sisters couldn't really figure out where I was coming from, but there were a few who were sympathetic, even if they did sound a little sarcastic.

"I think it's really great that you want to bring Nzingha care to the world, somebody has to save this big ol' nasty planet from itself."

Yeah, the sign says – "Dr. Nzingha Howard" – and I'm proud of myself, no matter what anybody says . . . ."

XXX    XXX

"I always wanted to be a doctor, always, since I was a little boy. Growing up in a small town in Southern California gave me the opportunity to see and deal with a lot of wildlife. Black bears prowled around, raided your trash cans if the lid wasn't tight and sometimes when the lid <u>was</u> tight.

Skunks, raccoons, possums, feral cats, wolves, coyotes. I can say, at this late date, that I was truly privileged to be a part of a living, outdoor zoo. I climbed up trees to look at hawk's eggs, dug down thru ant cities to see ants and how they lived.

My Mom and Dad were completely indulgent, 'til the afternoon I bought home this baby kitten I had found wandering around in the woods behind our home.

"Uhh, Jonathan, this is a bobcat cub, son. This animal's DNA, so far as me and your Mom is concerned, is designed to be out there, not in here. We don't think it's right or ethical to try to cultivate alien behavior into wild creatures. Take it back to where you found it, his mother is probably crazy from wondering what happened to her son.

"But, Dad, Mom, what happens if the animal's parents have moved on, found a new habitat?"

"Jonathan, trust me on this one; I'm your Mom. What do you think I would do if I lost you down at the mall? Do you think I would try to find out what happened to you, or not?"

"You'd try to find out, no doubt about it."

"Picture a bobcat Mom back there in the woods, looking for her cub, and you'll understand why we're asking you to take it back where it belongs . . . ."

"But, Mom, Dad, if the bobcat's parents are not there. What if the cub's parents have ....?

"Jonathan, we feel that it would be better for the bobcat cub to die in the wilderness, rather than live with us, with behavior patterns that are so alien to their culture."

Yes, Mom and Dad were wonderful mentors, ethical guides to where I was going. They didn't speak in proverbs or great, deep dark sentences, they simply explained things as they understood them. My Mom, for example, once explained – "Jonathan, think about how often you've heard the expression – "Shit happens" – ever thought seriously about – "Shit happens" -- ?

I had never given any serious thought to the expression – "Shit happens." Who would want to give a serious thought to what shit happens?

Mom spent the whole evenings explaining why shit was so important.

"Think about it, Jonathan, what comes out of you can offer an incredible amount of information about what's wrong with you."

Mom and Dad were definitely the catalysts for me going into the Holistic practice of Medicine. They weren't anti-Western, but they made it plain that they were pro-Eastern.

"Jonathan, I don't think we oughta close off any avenue to good health. Having said that, personally, I feel more inclined to being treated by someone who concerns himself/herself with my whole being, rather than someone who is only dealing with one section of my being, 'practicing' medicine. I've never heard anyone talk about 'practicing' acupuncture. You know what I mean?"

We had many of those kinds of sessions, many. By the time I was fifteen I was treating, or trying to treat everybody around me, literally. It became a running joke amongst my friends.

"Be careful about yawnin' around Jonathan, he'll start studying your tongue"

They had their jokes, made light hearted fun, but when they weren't feeling well, when something was bothering them, they came to me.

"Hey, Jonathan, know of any herbs I could take for this excess mucus in my throat?"

XXX     XXX

Dr. Jonathan Hoover folded his arms across his chest and stared out of the window into his backyard. A gorgeous autumn day in Southern California. Verona pulling weeds here and there, snipping bushes, coddling the roses in her garden. Hummingbirds flitting here and there, sipping nectar. Peace.

He replayed the conversation on his mental tape.

"Doc, I swear to you, I was there. I've never seen so many people working so hard in my whole life. . . ."

"Bob, what you're telling me is that you're no longer having pains in your lower . . .?"

"I'm not having any pains in my lower back. But what I'm also telling you is that the last three sessions took me Out There . . ."

"Out there?" He had practically ignored Robert "Bob" Bradford's declaration that he had been "Out There" before his – Dr. Anouska Mehta – counseling kicked in.

"Do not ignore your patient's reactions to your treatment, you can never tell when they might be telling you something you didn't know, or even suspected."

Robert "Bob" Bradford, lawyer. Detail oriented, analytical, somewhat impatient with people and circumstances that were not rational. Intense, suffered from migraines, lower back aches that were probably the results of too much mental tension. A two-pack a day smoker – "Yeah, I know it's no good for me. That's why I'm going to give it up . . . soon."

What was he? Six feet two, a hundred and sixty-five pounds, somewhat careless about what he ate.

"C'mon, Doc, who has time for more than a sandwich and a cuppa coffee? There's stuff to be done."

Robert "Bob" Bradford, from the Bradfords of Orange County, an overachiever from a family of Overachievers.

"Mom and Dad always stressed how important it was to make the family name glow. Martha, my older sister, obviously disregarded the family vibe and spent most of her life going in and out of rehab for various addictions. Maybe the pressure of being a Bradford was too much for her to deal with."

"Bob, I'm not a psychologist, but you said something to me during our last session that I found to be very, very interesting. You said that you had been 'Out There.' Want to give me a more detailed explanation of what you mean by that? Like I said, I'm not a psychologist, so I can't give you any interpretation of anything, but I'd certainly like to know what 'Out There' means.

XXX    XXX

"Well, as you know, if it hadn't been for Stella . . . ."

"Your wife."

"Yes, Stella my wife, if it hadn't been for her I wouldn't've come to you. 'Bob,' she told me, 'go see Dr. Hoover. Remember me complaining about the pain in my neck from that car accident last month? After those acupuncture sessions I feel about 80% better. He told me, during my first visit – 'this is not about miraculous healing or anything like that. What I'm going to do is 're-open the circuits,' in a manner of speaking, so that your body's natural healing agents will be able to flow more forcefully. The body is a truly awesome machine, all it needs is a little help, from time to time.'"

"I have to be honest with you, Doc, I just couldn't get with the idea of having needles stuck in my body to cure anything. Prior to coming to you, I did a little reading about acupuncture and stuff like that, of course I had some knowledge of what it was about, in a general way, but I have to confess, I was still skeptical . . . ."

"So, you've changed your mind and attitude about the subject?"

"Completely, 'specially after the last treatment."

"You spoke about going 'Out There,' please explain."

Robert Bradford was one of those perpetually serious people. He gave me a little smile from time to time. But he usually had a serious expression. On this occasion, his expression became more serious than usual.

"I don't quite know how to go about explaining this, or I should say I hope you won't think I've lost my mind . . . ."

"No need to be concerned about anything like that, Bob, just spool it out any way you want to."

Bob had been my last patient of the day. I could cut him a little slack, I had a two-hour window before I had to deal with a stack of forms. He slumped in the leather upholstered chair in front of my desk.

"It happened with the first session we had, Doc, the very first session . . . ."

16

I was beginning to feel slightly annoyed. Was Bob on some kind of drug that I didn't know about? Does being "Out There" mean being spaced, on drugs? I decided not to push him, to give him the space he seemed to need. When he opened up and started talking, like someone in a trance-like state, his voice had changed. He didn't sound like himself.

"It was as though I had floated into an abyss, a place where there was Nothing. I had never experienced <u>Nothing</u> before. I knew about it as a philosophy #101 term, but not as a reality. I was suddenly there and had no idea how I got there or why I was there. The floating sensation seemed to last for a loonng time. And then I stopped floating and found myself walking through a desert. All I could see for miles around me in every direction was huge mounds of sand, sand everywhere.

The sun was shining on me but it wasn't hot. More like a soothing light than hot. I had no idea where I was or where I was going and it didn't matter. I was 'Out There.' Maybe that's what my sub consciousness told me, said to me.

I can't say how long I walked, never hungry, never thirsty, never confused, angry, lonesome, fearful. I simply walked and started thinking – which God did this to me? Whose God is responsible for this, this thisness?

Why did I think of a God? I don't know. It just seemed, at the time, that there must be some Superior Beings in this place I was strolling through, and they had decided to show lil' ol' me how great and powerful they were.

Had to be Gods, and not <u>A</u> God. There were too many issues for one God to deal with, to be responsible for. Was I thinking, or was a meridian leading me into these thought patterns?

Suddenly, it was always suddenly, people materialized around me. No one spoke to me, asked me any questions. I couldn't say that we were walking fast or slow, thousands of us, but we were all moving in the same direction. We struggled a bit to get to the top of a giant wave of a sand dune and when we got to the top of the wave, when I got to the top, I stopped moving, stood in place and stared at a sight that it would be impossible to describe in detail.

In this huge valley in front of me, there were thousands of people, like the people around me, pushing, pulling huge stones into place. They were building a pyramid. I could tell it was a pyramid from the way it was shaping up. They looked like ants at work.

The people around me were on their way to work on this gigantic pyramid. They streamed forward, curling around me as though I were a rock in the middle of a shallow stream. I have no idea how long I stood there, staring at this incredible sight. I could see that the workers were Africans, their color validated that, but they weren't all sub Saharan black. As a matter of fact many of them were light walnut colored.

So, I was in Africa, in Egypt, where these giant pyramids were first built. . . ."

Bob paused for a long moment. Had he gone to sleep?

"Uhhh, Bob, is that it? That the end of the story?"

"No, Doc, that's only the beginning." He made another long pause.

"You don't think I'm making this up, do you, Doc?"

"No, Bob, I don't think you're making up anything. Go on."

"I don't know how long I stood there taking in the scene; it seemed like a long time. But I have to be honest and say that time seemed to accommodate the circumstances. If I stared at a group of workmen doing something over there, that I was interested in, it seemed like I could spend hours studying their movements, the stuff they were doing. However, if I looked at a bunch of people who were not doing anything interesting to me, I could get away from them with a hard glance or two.

I've never seen so many people work so hard in my life. It was quite easy to see that these people were being driven to work. The men who prowled around the workers carried whips and they used them whenever they felt like using them.

It was organized chaos in the best sense of the word. They were building a pyramid, or some pyramids, I couldn't really determine which. I had read enough, and seen enough stuff about ancient Egypt to know that I was witnessing the construction of some unique structures in the world.

The scale of things was incredible. It seemed impossible to believe that human beings were doing what they were doing. I knew, from my casual acquaintance with the subject, that many people had given credit to outer space creatures, extraterrestrials, for having created the pyramids.

Now I could give testimony of having seen the real deal, men at work, building the Egyptian pyramids from scratch. But what the hell was I doing there, and how did I get there?"

"Dan, I'm telling you – this guy seemed to think that I'd touched some sort of nerve in his subconscious, a meridian, a nerve that took him back to ancient times. 'Out There' is the way he put it."

"Did you?"

"Did I what?"

"Did you hit a meridian that took him back to ancient times?"

"Of course not, how could I? And where is it located? C'mon, Dan, we're talking seriously here."

"I am being serious. I'll be free after Tai Chi on Sunday morning. Why don't we get together and talk about this a lil' more?"

"What time?"

"We usually finish at ten o'clock…."

"Signal Hill, right?"

"Signal Hill, right."

"Uhhh, Jonathan, have you ever spoken to Verona about this?"

"Not a whisper. Remember Dr. Mehta's mantra?"

"In order for your patient to have confidence in you, you must not betray that confidence by blabbing their business all over the place, not even to your lawfully bewedded."

"Hahahhah, see you Sunday morning."

"Great! My best to CoCo…."

XXX     XXX

# CHAPTER 3

"How many years ago was that, that we had our stroll around the perimeters of Signal Hill? As Jonathan talked about his patient "Bob," his 'Out There' guy. It took a lot for me to restrain myself because I had a couple 'mystery stories' of my own to lay on him.

"Dan, I'm telling you exactly what 'Bob' told me. I have to admit, I thought the guy was hallucinating, or pulling my leg when he really got into his story. But it wasn't anything like that; he was simply telling me what had happened to him, where he went when he went 'Out there.'"

"Doc, I have to be honest with you, my interest in Egypt, past and present, was semi-nil."

This conversation/disclosure took place after our second session. We had reduced his lower back pains substantially; the focus now was on his migraines. In between times, this is what he told me.

"A day after I had witnessed the building of a pyramid, or pyramids, a tall, dark skinned Aristocrat tapped me on the shoulders and sign languaged to me that I should follow him. I followed him. What else could I do? Was I dreaming?

I could tell that he was Somebody by the way people reacted to our movement to, to wherever we were going. It was awesome, Doc, absolutely awesome."

I felt like a psychiatric fraud when I asked him – "What were the people's reactions?" -- I mean, let's face it. What would I learn from their reactions? Reactions to what?

"The reactions were reverent, very respectful. Thousands of people opened an avenue for us to walk through. It was like an ancient Hollywood movie, where the sea splits open to allow Charlton Heston or somebody to drive a chariot through. I'm sure I didn't walk, I floated. That was the feeling.

Later, as though I had wandered in from a hike through a sea of people, I was taken to a small palace. Yes, a palace. And given luxurious treatment. Gently stripped, bathed in perfumed waters, dressed in beautifully made linen clothes, my feet placed in beautifully made leather sandals, fed delicious food.

Strange as it might seem, none of what was happening to me had to be explained, it seemed quite natural.

Later that evening my guide Gamal ('handsome') took me to his palace/home to a party. It was a truly beautiful scene, Doc, truly beautiful. The women were absolutely gorgeous, the music was wonderful, the dances were incredible. Can you see the scene, Doc?"

I was tempted to tell him – no, Bob, I can't see the scene, just to keep things on a realistic plane. But the truth of the matter was that I could see the matter vividly. I knew a little about ancient Egypt.

"Yes, Bob, I can see the scene. I can see it . . . ." And it was true; the scene resonated in my brain. I wasn't an Egyptologist or anything like that, but I definitely knew a lot more about life in ancient Egypt than he did, and he was talking to me about what it was like to be there, Right Now. It was definitely kinda crazy, on one level, but not really crazy on a hundred other levels. I was absolutely fascinated.

"Bob, let me get this straight. Are you telling me that, as a result of your acupuncture, you were able to trip off to ancient Egypt?"

"Well, not exactly, Doc. Actually, the way Gamal . . . ."

"Your guide?"

"Yes, Gamal, my guide. The way he explained it to me was like this – "The Lord Imhotep is, as the whole world knows, one of the greatest magicians on the planet. As well as being a great physician. He is also Chancellor of the King of Egypt, Doctor, First in line after the King of Upper Egypt, Administrator of the Great Palace, Hereditary nobleman, High Priest of Heliopolis, Builder, Chief Carpenter, Chief Sculptor and Maker of Vases in Chief."

Maybe I sounded a bit irreverent when I said; "sounds like Imhotep is a Renaissance Man . . . ."

"A Renaissance Man". "I don't know this term," he said, "but I'm certain that this is something that Lord Imhotep would like to ask questions about . . . ."

"Renaissance Man," I had to remember that I was somewhere in the 27$^{th}$ century B.C. (c. 2650-2600 B.C.) and that the "Renaissance" was yet to come. Concerning me, being Out There and acupuncture.

To be honest I would never be able to say that you put a needle in a specific place and that took me 'Out.' No, it wasn't anything like that, but I do think that the acupuncture put me in a state of mind to be able to go where I went.

Gamal supplied me with some interesting information that I'm still trying to process – he told me, "You must understand that Lord Imhotep is a very great magician and he is able to do things that ordinary men dare not dream about."

"So, Gamal, my friend, you're saying that I'm here because Imhotep, Lord Imhotep, has used some magical means to bring me here?"

"I cannot say because I do not know. I am fascinated by magic but I do not understand it."

"Well, let's just say that Lord Imhotep used magical means to bring me here. Why me?"

"Why not you?"

Why not me? That thought caromed in my skull for hours. For years.

## XXX    XXX

"I made two trips to Egypt before I was taken to see Lord Imhotep. The first time I was there I spent a year just absorbing the vibes of the place, sightseeing, simply being there."

"Bob, you're telling me that you left my acupuncture table and went to Egypt for a year? I only left you in that room for thirty minutes."

Poor Bob, the only thing he could do was shrug his shoulders. I was completely puzzled. And so was he.

"I know, Doc, I know it sounds weird but that's what happened. I'm not making any of this up. It has to do with something that might be called a time warp of some kind.

It seemed that my acupuncture treatment gave me the right state of mind, or whatever you want to call it, for me to go 'Out There.'"

"I see what you mean now, about being 'Out There.' Go on."

"Yeah, Out There, another world. I had no sense of whirling through space or anything like that. I simply went from here to there. That half hour morphed into a year, that's all I know.

"That's what happened the first time. I wanted to talk to you about the experience, but I was so tripped out, so afraid that you would think that I was on an LSD trip or something. I just couldn't talk about it, to you or anyone else."

"What happened the second time?"

Once again I witnessed a change come over Bob. His voice slipped to a deeper tone and this trance-like state came over him. Was I talking with someone who had acquired multiple personalities?

"I was taken by my guide, Gamal, who had become my friend, to visit Lord Imhotep. First off, I must say that I think Lord Imhotep is the wisest man I ever met in my entire life. He lived in a grand palace, with many servants and all that, but I didn't have the feeling that he was impressed by his surroundings, his royal environment.

We were ushered through the palace by Lord Imhotep's right hand man; I guess we would call him the Maitre d' of the establishment. Huge, beautiful rooms, cool, despite the Egyptian heat. I had watched noblemen and women go down on their knees and crawl up to the throne-chairs of high ranking officials and I was prepared to do the same 'til Gamal whispered to me – 'you don't have to do that, Lord Imhotep is not in favor of that . . . .'

Doc, you have to imagine the size of these Egyptian palace rooms. The palace I lived in was the size of a small football field. The size of Lord Imhotep's palace was twice that size. I expected him to be seated on a throne-chair, looking as stiff as one of those statuettes in the French Louvre, the British Museum, the Chicago Institute of Embalmed Egyptians, or whoever/whenever.

Nothing like that. He was wayyy over there when we were ushered into his living quarters, if you can imagine a small football field as living quarters. He was shooing a collection of children away from him as we entered.

"His children," trusty Gamal whispered, "he has many. Remember you will <u>not</u> crawl on your knees into his presence."

I did a casual measurement of the space that separated us and came to the conclusion that I would've died of arthritis or de-hydration, if I had been forced to crawl across the space that separated us. Imhotep solved the problem immediately. After he had dismissed his children, he strolled over to where we were; me, Gamal, my guide, and Amun, his 'maitre d'.

He was a small man, about the size of Mahatma Gandhi, with the same coloring, but minus Gandhi's nose and mustache. He welcomed us with a smile and signed for us to follow him. We followed. He led us to a beautifully marbled table for four off to the side of the huge room. Once we were at the table, he announced, "I am Imhotep, welcome to my home . . . ."

What could I say?

"Uhh, pleased to meet you, Sir, my name is Robert Bradford."

"Yes, I know – please be seated."

The minute we sat down two servants eased into the room; one with a huge plate of grapes, bananas, and other fruits. A beautiful girl swayed into the room with a tray balanced on her head. She carried a huge pitcher of juice, lemonade actually, and three beautiful drinking bowls. Lord Imhotep poured drinks into our bowls. And dribbled a libation for the gods.

I had been on the scene long enough to know that people didn't just jump into things, it wasn't all business first. We sipped our lemonades. I studied the Lord Imhotep without trying to be too obvious about it. The thing that struck me most profoundly was the sense of serenity about the room.

This was the second most powerful man in the land (after the pharaoh), but there was no big time ego on display. I didn't have the feeling that he had a 'master complex' or any of that. His sense of cool actually made me relax. I was literally seduced by the ambience of the scene. You know what I mean, Doc?"

"Bob, you're making it perfectly clear, please go on. . . ."

I had decided to cancel whatever else I had on the backburner in order to hear Bob's story, no matter how long it took.

"We had one big time interruption during our 'meeting.' A man with several long scrolls under his arm was ushered into Lord Imhotep's presence.

He was profusely apologetic about interrupting, but it was obviously an emergency situation. Lord Imhotep excused himself.

"This is very important; I must attend to this before it becomes a big problem."

What could I say? The whole scene struck me as being, what would you call it? Surreal? One of the designers of the Sakkara pyramids (I found out later) was being consulted, while I was on the scene, munching on succulent black skinned grapes, sipping a tart lemonade.

The ever present servants pulled in a huge table about fifty yards away from our space, just close enough for me to witness the master architect at work. The man who had brought the scrolls unrolled them on the table. I assumed that they were architectural plans/maps or whatever.

Lord Imhotep pointed this way, zigzagged his right finger from here to there on the scroll that was sprawled on the table in front of him. No hesitation, no dawdling, that was something that I can recall without effort. It was a 'here', do this! There, do that!' kind of thing.

The guy who had interrupted our meeting re-rolled his scrolls, looking extremely grateful, as he bowed-bowed-bowed his way out of Lord Imhotep's presence. Lord Imhotep joined us at the table with a sly smile on his face and a mischievous gleam in his eyes.

"Don't let anybody tell you that building pyramid is an easy business."

I didn't know what to say. On one hand I felt that I was witnessing ancient history, but in another way, I felt that I was a part of that history. I was a little confused, to put it bluntly. Lord Imhotep leaned toward me after he rejoined us.

"You're wondering how it is that you can understand what I'm saying, because you're only speaking your language, and we're only speaking our language. Is that on your mind?"

I shrugged and gave a dumb nod. What else could I do?

"Well, Bob, you must understand that I am a magician and that there are things I can do that other men do not even think about doing..."

He pronounced my name, "Bab," not "Bob." I probed.

"Lord Imhotep, I can understand that you are a magician, Sir, I can truly understand that you are. And an engineering genius, and all the other things that you are. But I can't understand how you have made it possible for me to understand your language and for you to understand my language. Can you please explain that?"

"I could, but I won't. Simply let me say this – I'm making it possible for us to speak to each other, using my magic. You notice that you do not understand anything that certain people are saying to you, correct?"

It didn't take more than a moment to reflect on his statement. I could hear/understand Gamal and Lord Imhotep, but the general population was incomprehensible. Lord Imhotep solved the problem.

"Bab, I'm making it possible for you to speak to the people you need to speak with while you are with us. I'm making this possible by magical means. Do you have a problem with that?"

"Magical means." What did that mean?

"Lord Imhotep, I have to ask you, what does 'magical means' mean?"

He looked slightly irritated for a few moments, as though my question was an irritant, something that anyone should be able to understand. But he didn't bite into me, the way a lot of others would've done. He explained; "Bab, let me be perfectly clear to you, 'magical means' may have disappeared, or may have acquired a different meaning/connotation in your era. You know what I'm sayin'?"

No bullshit, Doc, I laughed out loud when I heard him say, "You know what I'm sayin'?" It was so modern so hip hoppish. He had used it for effect and the effect was achieved. He smiled slyly.

"'Magical means' means exactly that, for us at this time and place. I suspect that something has been lost over the centuries.

Please tell us, how do you define 'magical means?'

I suddenly felt like someone who had been called on to explain something that I barely understood, to someone who seemed capable of understanding damned near everything, including how to build pyramids to order. It took me a few seconds to collect myself. I wanted to give a truthful response.

"Well, first off, Lord Imhotep, we tend to think of magic as a collection of clever tricks, things that people can be taught to do...."

"So, magicians are made not born. Is that what you're saying? Bab?"

Made, not born. O my God, I'd never thought of anything like that. I felt confused. Lord Imhotep gently eased me along – "Speak from your heart, from experience, Bab. Speak honestly . . . ."

I took a deep breath and spoke . . . .

"Lord Imhotep, what I am going to say to you concerning magic, what I understand about it, coming from where I come from, is that it's all about results. What I mean by that is that the magician will do an unusual number of things and he/she will produce an unusual number of results.

Clever people can be taught to do magical tricks. The cleverer they are, the cleverer the tricks will be. I don't think that we expect to have this person understand that person's language by 'magical means.' You know what I'm sayin'?"

I wish I had had a camera to capture the expression on Lord Imhotep's face. He seemed somewhat amused, but puzzled at the same time.

"So, you're saying that there are no practical applications of magic, just people doing tricks?"

I didn't feel that he was trying to mouse trap me or anything like that; I simply felt that he wanted an honest answer from me. I gave the question some serious thoughts for a few beats.

"Sir, I've never given this matter a lot of thought, but I would have to say, based on my experience, that magic, in the way it is presented or done where I come from . . . means 'just people doing tricks.' What else could I say?"

He settled back in his chair, tented his hand under his chin and seemed to be meditating for a few minutes. He sounded sad when he spoke.

"That's not a good thing. Your people are missing one of the greatest gifts the gods have ever given us. Magic is all around us, begging us to make use of it."

"Is this magic that you speak of available to everyone?"

Once again that sly smile slid in place.

"No, not to everyone."

"Then, Sir, may I ask who it is available to?"

"It is available to magicians, to those who have mastered the art of magic. Come, let's take a walk in the garden, it will be cool this time of the afternoon. We have a great deal to talk about."

I have to admit, my head was spinning a little bit as we followed Lord Imhotep into the palace gardens. He had opened up a door in my mind. Magic could be used like a hammer, a saw, a computer, a tool.

XXX    XXX

"Well Dan, what do you think of it, so far . . . .?"

Dr. Daniel Lane II stared down onto buildings, the streets, the cars whizzing around, ant/people going from place to place. Signal Hill was one of his favorite places in the world. From the Pacific Ocean over there to the buildings of downtown Los Angeles. The panoramic view gave him a feeling of ownership. He recalled the many times he had driven David and Heather up to this hill on balmy summer evenings.

One of his pet jokes was to stand between his eight-year son and his seven-year old daughter, place his hands on their small shoulders and announce, in dramatic tones.

"Just think, my children, when you grow up . . . none of this will belong to you."

Years later they had stood in the same spot and announced, in comic/tandem – "Just think, Dad, we're all grown up now, and none of this belongs to us."

"So, Bob's story makes you smile. I guess that's a good sign."

"No, it wasn't the story that makes me smile; it was the memory of the times I used to bring David and Heather up here.

Concerning this guy's story? I think it's absolutely incredible. Where is he now?"

"I'm coming to that, I'm coming . . . .

"The Lord Imhotep's garden. First off I noticed that there was every kind of shady tree you could think of. Gorgeous bushes literally sprouting dazzling, colorful flowers. Beautiful birds fluttered from tree to tree. Carvings were placed strategically for maximum effect. I counted a dozen gardeners snipping, pruning, planting, re-planting here and there.

We strolled on wide stone pathways thru the gardens. There were acres and acres of green all around us and it was like the man, serene, mellow. He asked, almost shyly. "Bab, would you like to see where I got to do my most serious meditations?"

"Yes Sir, I would very much like to see . . . ."

Amun, Lord Imhotep's "maître d'" and my guide/friend, Gamal, followed us, walking ten yards behind. I felt, for the umpteenth time, that I had to be dreaming.

I was tempted to do several things at the same time; pick up a pad and pen and start taking notes. Two, open my desk drawer and pull out this miniature Japanese recorder. Three, put Bob on hold while I gathered up a half dozen people to validate what I was hearing.

At the end of the day, as the saying goes, my sense of wonder at what he was saying held me in place. I was literally glued to the edge of my seat listening to this, this, this unusual story.

"We walked for about five minutes through a dense section of the gardens before we came to a clearing, and in the clearing there was a small hut built of sun dried adobe. It reminded me of some of the adobe homes you see in the poor sections of Southern Mexico."

"This is my sanctuary," he said, as he led me up the path to the entrance. "This is the house I was born in."

The whole thing almost blew me away. Imhotep, the second most powerful man in this land was showing me his origin, his birth place.

"This is where I feel most at ease," he almost whispered as we entered the hut. You would have to be thinking generously to call it a house. Hut is a more accurate description.

"I came from these circumstances." It seemed that he was speaking to himself, reminding himself of where he came from. It only took a few minutes to complete a tour of the inside of the hut before he led me into a small courtyard. It was, for me, like a claustrophobic relief.

"I had this courtyard placed here because I realized, early on, that many people were having 'problems' dealing with the tightness of the place I came from."

We sat down at a picnic table-like bench, upholstered by the skins of cheetahs and other rare animals. I could imagine a bunch of my friends ragging me – "Rare animal hides, Bob?! C'mon man, you've got more consciousness than that."

I felt the emotional pull of their distant arguments, but I had to remind myself – hey, I'm a guest; I can't tell my host what to do, or how to do it. And besides, none of these animals have been hunted into extinction, the way we did it.

The servants swayed onto the scene with more juices, fruits, smiles.

"They like you," Lord Imhotep whispered to me.

"But why?" I whispered back.

"Ra only knows," he whispered back, his sly smile pasted in place. Once again I was alerted to the fact that I wasn't in a one dimensional place, a one layered spot. Stuff was so deep.

Gamal and Lord Imhotep's maître d' Amun joined us at the picnic table. They were there, but they were very deferential, as though they were on the scene to serve their master. There was no friendly buddy-buddy stuff. If anything, I was the loose cannon on the scene. Can you see the scene, Doc?"

I don't know why he had to keep asking me that question. Maybe it was his way of reaffirming his own inner vision, of validating what had happened to him.

"Bob, or should I call you 'Bab'"?

He fed on my humor, smiled a bit more than usual.

"Please feel free to call me 'Bab', that reminds me of who I was."

I couldn't quite get what he meant by that, so I circled around behind it.

"Bob, please rest assured that I can see the scene, you paint a very vivid picture. You're seated at a picnic table in the courtyard of the great Lord Imhotep, the courtyard is located next to this peasant hut where he was born. Obviously he had transported this humble hut into the midst of his majestic circumstances, as a reminder of his humble beginnings."

"Yes, yes, that's exactly what he told me . . . ."

"And the guide he had assigned to you, this guy Gamal is there and the Lord Imhotep's main man, his maitre d' you called him, is there, and the servants are serving you goodies. Is that the scene?"

"That's the immediate scene, no doubt about it, but there was so much more happening that it would take a book to describe it. . . ."

"Why don't we just stick with the outstanding details?"

Once again, Bob's attitude changed, his voice tone went into another level, he changed into another person right in front of me. I don't mean physically, but in a way I can't find the words to describe. It was like listening to someone from another time.

XXX    XXX

# CHAPTER 4

"BAB, I MUST ASK YOU – are people still making war upon each other?"

"Yes Sir, I'm sorry to say that people are still making war upon each other."

He shook his head slowly, sadness registering with each motion.

"I can't make myself believe that this is so, the future should've learned from the past – 'war is not the answer.'"

Lord Imhotep was constantly spooking me out with these futuristic remarks – "Know what I'm sayin'?" "Everything is Everything," "Now is the time," "Bright moments," "Maybe yes, maybe no."

There in this small courtyard behind the hut of Lord Imhotep's birth, I felt that I was being reborn. Really reborn, not physically but intellectually and psychologically.

"So, they say that all of this knowledge, this intelligence, this magical spirituality, these monuments cannot be attributed to Africans, to Africa, to us, because of racism. Please, Bab, please explain, I cannot understand . . . ."

"Doc, can you understand what Lord Imhotep was asking me? Explain why Anglo racism on earth, I can't think of a better term, was going to explain that the Egyptian pyramids could not have possibly been constructed by Africans, 'by us, a people established in the northeast corner of the Motherland of humanity.' I have to admit, I stumbled a bit."

"Lord Imhotep," I felt at ease with calling him "Lord Imhotep" because everything that surrounded him indicated that he was a lord.

"Lord Imhotep, you've asked me to try to explain one of the most complicated most complex problems that 'non-Egyptians' have ever had to deal with. I will do my best to give you the most honest answer I can give you.

The 'non-Egyptians' on our planet, who've always felt that they were under a racial siege because they were a minority on Earth, an aggressive minority, but still a minority, went at the Egyptian miracles, the pyramids, big time. They wanted to discredit the people of Africa for creating the pyramids because they felt that it would be giving the Africans who are responsible for creating these incredible monuments too much credit."

Lord Imhotep looked startled and then amused. His by now sly smile appeared.

"But, Bab, the only thing any sensible person has to do, dating from now, to where you came from, is to look at the map, my map or your map, to see that our land is in the northeastern corner of Africa. What's the problem?"

"Lord Imhotep, the problem is a white problem. After having developed an inferiority complex over a period of centuries, they didn't have a vested interest in giving grand theft appreciation to a bunch of Africans, no matter how sophisticated, for creating what you've created here."

He tented his hands under his chin, a gesture he used when he was thinking, considering something.

"I don't quite understand 'grand theft,' what does that mean?"

"Uhh, it's both a legal term and a slang term, it indicates that someone has done a big crime."

"Ahhah, I see, said the blind man."

We shared a laugh. The man had a dry sense of humor and obviously liked to play word games. We sat in the cool courtyard and sipped our lemonades, not speaking, just enjoying the breezes that came in soft waves.

"Bab, I have invited a few friends to my home to meet you this evening, is that cool with you?' He had masterful timing.

I almost spilled my lemonade answering – "Yes, yes, yessir, Lord Imhotep, I would love to meet your friends."

"Come, there is time to take a small nap and freshen up. Clothes have been brought here from your home."

"Thank you, I appreciate that."

We retraced our steps back to his palace before he spoke again.

"Oh, incidentally, our great Lord and Master, Pharaoh Djoser would like for you to have dinner with him tomorrow evening . . . Looks like your social calendar is filling up."

"The Pharaoh himself? Wowww. . . ."

Imhotep smiled at my enthusiasm as he led me to my suite of rooms. A shower, a nap and a meeting with his friends. I was really feeling good about all of this, but I still had this feathery feeling in my guts, that the whole thing was an "incredible dream and that the rug would be pulled from underneath my feet any minute. . . ."

He paused for so long after he made that statement that I felt compelled to prompt him a bit.

"So, Bob, your man, Lord Imhotep, has invited a few friends into his home to meet with you. What was that like?"

He surged back into his narrative as though I had stabbed him with a rusty acupuncture needle.

"O my God! What was it like? My friend, guide Gamal had given a party for me and I was definitely pleased by that. The absolutely gorgeous women, the music, the dancing, the delicious foods, the things that intoxicated me so delightfully.

Well, first off, this was a scene happening at Lord Imhotep's house, castle, palace. He could use his hut-in-the-woods as a reference point, but, as Lord Imhotep, as the second <u>most</u> <u>most</u> <u>High</u>, there could be no such thing as a casual evening at Master Imhotep's place.

He introduced me to noble after noble, most of royal blood. "Lord Seth, please know 'Bab,' our visitor from Beyond . . . ."

I tripped on that at the beginning of my introduction to the elite of Memphis society, the stronghold of Imhotep cult behavior, as a tricky intro. "Our visitor from Beyond."

From Beyond where? Well, what did that mean? It didn't take us very long to get off into it. It didn't take long for us to begin to understand/deal with things, stuff that they were fueled on.

"Please, sir, tell us who you are and why you're here?"

"I beg you, sir, to direct your question to our Lord Imhotep, I can only say to you that I am a creature from there, and not from here . . . ."

Lord Imhotep, speaking almost like a presidential press secretary, spooled the question around so cleverly that I found myself wondering what the person who had asked the question could get from his circum-navigationalized answer.

I think, it was at that point, that I began to relate to the idea of how much back then is like right now. The questions flew loud and clear – "What will you do with the people you discover, the 'primitive' people on the scene, who have been there, wherever, thousands of years before you've 'discovered' them?"

"I think we will do the same thing you've done with the folks you've colonized south of here, the Nubians, the Dogons and others. We will conquer them and enslave them, physically and psychologically. That's what our history has been. We will, eventually, discover a way to bleed them for money."

A large number wanted to push the slavery issue off to the side and deal with purely "techno issues." I pressed the question "Robots are ahead in your history, how will you deal with them, as human, or non-human beings."

Some of the beings on the scene couldn't quite relate to "robots."

"What does this mean – robots?"

Lord Imhotep pushed it to the curb by saying – "Robots, artificial beings, things that we have created to help us out, who receive no pay or health care benefits, who have no citizenship rights . . . ." He clearly understood the future of robotic stuff.

His answer seemed to seal up that hole for a few beats. How many people were on the scene? Two hundred? Three hundred? And they were a seriously curious bunch. The questions came hot 'n heavy, but I didn't have the feeling that they were trying to do one-ups-manship-stuff on me. Well, I guess I should qualify that because there were a few who were obviously hostile.

"Please, tell us, what is the most important technological thing of this future that you come from?"

That was a toughie. I had to waffle a bit.

"I'm sorry, sir, I can't really place my finger on 'the most important technological thing.' There have been so many that were, are important. Someone might say, 'the computer.' Someone else would say 'nuclear energy,' or cameras and cellphones, space vehicles, the cure for cancer, the cure for blindness and so on and so forth."

Doc, please understand that this wasn't taking place in a vacuum; people were eating, drinking, having a good time, I was having a good time. But like I said earlier, there were a few who were obviously hostile. One of them, a snake-faced man with heavy make up around his eyes, asked; "So, you have been with us for a while, long enough for you to see that our civilization is superior to yours. What do you have that is better than what we have?"

It could've been a straight forward enough question, but there was an edge to it, a hint that I was from the inferior future. I had to be careful; I didn't want to offend my host or his guests.

"I wouldn't like to even suggest that where I'm coming from is any greater, more superior to anything that I've found here. To be absolutely honest with you, I can't say that I know enough about where I'm coming from to be able to compare it to your civilization."

The snake-faced man looked puzzled and then a sneer lit up his expression, as though he had trapped me in some way.

"So, you're saying that you're bringing us nothing from where you come from?"

"No, sir, I'm not saying that at all. What I'm saying is that the place I come from is so huge, so diverse, that no one person could/can possibly master all the facets of our world. There are people who know tons of stuff about astronomy, isometrics, psychology, music, of one kind or another, gymnastics, aerodynamics, mathematics, philosophy, I could go on and on and on.

I couldn't say that I'm bringing you superior knowledge about all of those areas, no, I couldn't do that."

"Well, what do you know about something?" Mr. Snake-face looked pissed.

"I'm a lawyer, perhaps I can say that I know a little about criminal law. I didn't say corporate law, that's another can of worms altogether . . . hahhahhah . . . ."

Lord Imhotep whispered – "That was very good Bab." "Mr. Snake-face" wasn't finished with me.

"What law is better than the Pharaoh's laws?"

Now I felt I was on solid ground, I could cope with "Mr. Snakeface's" snarky questions. I was a lawyer, degreed.

"Sir, I can't say that I know enough about the Pharaoh's laws to be able to make an assessment of his laws on any intelligent comment.

However, I can say this, if you're willing to listen to me?"

I saw Lord Imhotep's sly smile out of the corner of my left eye. Evidently I had scored a point with him, and a number of others. But I could also see that "Mr. Snakeface" had a collection of people who were behind his "grinning" at the impertinent stranger. So, what's different between then and now?

"Speak, I'm willing to listen." "Mr. Snakeface" replied to my question with a sarcastic curl of his full lips. So, now you're willing to listen. So, what should I say? I was a criminal attorney, a guy who defended criminals, people who were accused/had been accused of crimes. I decided to go with the flow.

"First off, let me say that I have learned, since I've been here, that Egypt has the most advanced system of laws in the world, the era we're in. Compared to many other parts of the world, as many of you know, the rights of women to have equal access to judgments is a part of your legal system. We know that property can be equally divided between male and female heirs. Women are granted full rights to own and bequeath property, file lawsuits, and bear witness in court proceedings without the authority of their fathers or husbands . . . ."

"You said you know nothing about the Pharaoh's laws!" Some witty type called out. I turned to face in his direction with my answer.

"I don't know anything about the Pharaoh's laws, but I do know a little about the history of this great land, and the history tells us that the working class here has rights. Even slaves are allowed to own property under certain circumstances."

I saw heads nod around me, including a number of people who were serving food and drinks, who might've been slaves.

"Basic human rights are respected here. And compared to the rest of the world around you, Egypt is, could be considered a bright light in the darkness.

I had to pause 'cause I didn't really know where I wanted to take this. I hadn't prepared a brief. One of 'Mr. Snakeface's entourage helped matters along."

"So, it seems that you've been allowed to return here, from there, and you simply tell us what we already know. We want to know what you've found out that we don't know. Work on that!"

I assumed that "work on that!" meant, "awright Mr. Thang, show us your stuff." I was up to it. I felt a momentary tinge of nervousness because I didn't have a well prepared, well documented brief, but what the hell . . . I took a deep breath.

"I would have to say that one of the greatest defenses against false accusations is that we, I'm stressing <u>we</u>, <u>we</u> have evolved a system of justice that says, unequivocally, that the accused is assumed to be innocent until proven guilty.

Here, in this great land of Egypt, of the Pharaohs, the opposite is assumed to be true, that the accused is assumed to be guilty until proven innocent."

The entire gathering was completely silent (after my comments had been translated to those people Imhotep, Lord, had been entitled to understand what I had said) for a few minutes.

"Why would someone accuse someone of a crime, if they were not guilty of that crime?" I had a logical answer on top.

"Why do human beings do what they do? Why don't we behave ourselves in a human way?"

Lord Imhotep, his wisdom be praised in the middle of a developing debate, mounted a small platform and announced in a velvet cool voice.

"Alright now, that's enough of that. Let's partay . . . ."

And that's the way that session ended, I was about to get off into what a criminal attorney does. Why shouldn't a person be considered innocent until proven guilty? I had to force myself to remember how long it took that concept to ice up. Meanwhile, as the "partay" bloomed, I found myself facing one of the most beautiful female creatures I had ever seen.

I didn't have to have anyone tell me that this girl-woman was a royal person, I could see it in the way she carried herself. Lord Imhotep gripped me gently by the left elbow and moved me around the room, meeting and speaking with people.

"You did well in your exchange with Prince Menkaure," someone said. I acknowledged the compliment with a little bow.

"Yes, Bab, you did do well," Lord Imhotep reaffirmed, "but I must caution you to be alert about Prince Menkaure, he is the kind of person who takes many things too seriously. Incidentally, the beautiful girl that you've been staring at is his youngest daughter. Her name is Senet. Come, let's have a bowl of wine with blue lotus petals, it will bring you blissful feelings."

Senet was Prince "Snakeface's" daughter. That information stunned me for a moment and then you were back in the room, gently removing these needles from different areas of my body. I was back. Or could I ever return?

XXX     XXX

It wasn't easy to be back, to return. Here from there. Dr. Hoover advised me to try to slowly re-orient myself.

"Bob, look, it's quite obvious that you've had some sort of psychic experience that has affected you deeply. I don't want to try to get in behind that because I wasn't there; but, based on what you've told me about your first and second visits to Lord Imhotep, I would like to suggest that you chill out for a few days, do a lot of thinking, and put things into perspective. What do you think?"

I agreed that doing a lot of thinking, putting things into perspective would be a good idea.

"Great! We'll see you again on, the . . . uhhh 6th of July. The migraines gone?"

"Seems that I've almost forgotten about them, Doc, with so much other stuff on my mind. But I'll take your advice . . . ."

I took Dr. Hoover's advice. I did a lot of thinking. I didn't want to remain married to Stella that was one of the more bizarre conclusions that came out of two weeks of hard thinking. I think I surprised myself when I arrived at <u>that</u> conclusion.

I didn't want to remain married to Stella. Why? Well, number one, I wasn't in love with Stella. I doubt if I was ever in love with Stella. Her mind maybe, but not totally who she was. We had met in law school, upward bound attorneys, destined to make tons of money, live a rich life. But love, I think not. We had the obligatory child, a boy named Anthony, and settled into a comfortable, brief-by-brief style of life. The dough rolled in, paying for our law school debts 'n all that, but love? Love gored me in the heart, or wherever love gores you, or strikes you, when it happens.

I fell in love with Senet. An Egyptian princess in my dreams. I went around feeling like a schizophrenic. Dr. Hoover had advised me to "put things in perspective." I was more than willing to do that, but the perspective kept shifting. I had been there, which furnished me a perspective that few modern people could possible imagine.

"Why me, Lord Imhotep?'

"Why not you, Bab? Please, just go with the flow. Those of us who've been nurtured by the Nile understand that better than most people."

Perspective. There was no flooding Nile in my life, spreading rich, productive soil. I was harnessed to a system, to systems that depended on unnatural perspectives. I was a criminal attorney, working for the Department of Justice.

It was an Orwellian-double-speak operation, guaranteed to confuse any poor applicant for a fair trial, a colored applicant for a fair trial, anyone who didn't have the proper money to nourish the systematic/neurotic application of "just-us."

I dreamt about Senet, about what our life would be like, could be like. I had to shake my head, to wake myself up every night before my next visit to Dr. Hoover. Stella took notice of my night sweats, my emotional gibberish in the middle of the night.

"Bob, are you o.k.?"

"Yeah, yeah, I guess so . . . ."

"So, when is your next appointment with Dr. Hoover?"

"Day after tomorrow."

## XXX    XXX

"Truth be told, as Dr. Hoover dabbed alcohol on all the acupuncture points he was going to tap his needles into, I felt like someone getting ready to take a looonnng trip. Dr. Hoover gave me a real funny look when I said – "Goodbye, Doc."

"I had never heard a patient say anything like that before . . . ."

I can recall that patient that was the one who got away . . . .

'C'mon, Dan, joke if you wasn't to, but just think about what you would feel like if you returned to a room where you had left a patient and there was no one there."

"Sorry, Jonathan, didn't mean to make light of things. I can remember the newspaper headlines – 'Alternative Health Professional Loses Patient.' They're the ones who tried to make fun of things,"

"Yeah, they had a field day. It was the tabloid newspaper-comedy hour. Dr. Jonathan Hoover, alternative medicine man, gives acupuncture treatment to patient. Patient disappears."

Dr. Mehta requested/called me in for a "consultation."

"Now, please understand me clearly, I understand that you are a fully qualified physician, definitely credited to hang your shingle out as a graduate of SoHMAA, but it is <u>not</u> desirable for our organization, for you, to have the kind of ludicrous publicity you've received – 'Alternative Health Professional Loses Patients' -- that is not the kind of publicity SoHMAA wants or desires. Are you getting me, Jonathan? Dr. Hoover."

"Loud 'n clear, Dr. Mehta, loud 'n clear."

"So, what happened to this patient that you are supposed to have lost, as a result of your acupuncture session?"

"I can't say, Dr. Mehta, I don't know."

XXX     XXX

"If I recall correctly, there was an over-sensationalized investigation made about what had happened in your office . . . ."

"You got that right. I was 'invited' to police headquarters to give a complete statement about what I know. I told them and I quote – 'I administered the appropriate acupuncture procedures for Mr. Robert Bradford. The procedure was supposed to last for approximately thirty-forty minutes. When I returned to Mr. Bradford's space, he was not there.

I left the space where I had given Mr. Robert Bradford's acupuncture treatments, to the receptionist's desk: I asked; 'Maria, did Mr. Bradford leave the hospital?'"

"No, Dr. Hoover, I don't have any record of anyone leaving the hospital this afternoon."

"Did you see Mr. Bradford leaving the hospital, either legally or illegally?"

"No, sir, I am very meticulous about who comes and goes. I can say, and I'm 100% sure; I did <u>not</u> see Mr. Bradford leave this facility. But why would we deny him the privilege of leaving the facility? He was not here under the stress of any particular life threatening element."

I went 'round and 'round for a few weeks. The mystery simply compounded itself.

XXX     XXX

# CHAPTER 5

IT TOOK A WHILE, BUT the whole business gradually died a natural death. I thank God that the American psyche doesn't seem to be geared or predisposed to hang on to things for very long. A few of my patients faded off of the scene as a result of what happened, but the majority stuck with me. Mrs. Peabody put it this way . . . .

"See here, you're an excellent physician, why should you be considered guilty of anything just because some nut brain decides to go into hiding? You've helped me get over my lower back pain, that's what's important to me. All of this other stuff is pure crap. Pardon my French."

"C'mon, Jonathan, don't keep me in suspense. What happened to Bob, to your patient?"

"I'm almost there. As you may recall, the Robert Bradford file became a cold case. That is to say, no one seemed to care about what happened to Bob after a period of years. Well, I shouldn't say no one – his son Anthony checked with me periodically."

"Dr. Hoover, this is Anthony Bradford . . . ."

What could I say to him? Son, I don't know what happened to your Dad. I don't know where he is. What else could I say?

Mrs. Bradford, a youngish looking forty-two-year-old blonde, got a divorce on grounds of desertion and re-married a week after the divorce came through. Anthony, the son, sort of wandered around for a while, but eventually found himself as a top of the line designer, specializing in men's clothes of the future.

"The future, Dr. Hoover, that's where it's at, the future. The past is dead, we have to give it a decent burial and move on."

I found no need to argue with the young man. I continued to do what my heart and training urged me to do. Things were going along "swimmingly," as the Brits say, when I received this ten-page letter at home. It was in ancient Egyptian script, on papyrus. The return address in the upper left hand corner said – "Bob/Saqquara, Egypt. It was exactly twelve years after "Bob's" disappearance. I had to take it down to the Egyptological Section of the Museum to have it deciphered. They were freaked out, to put it coolly.

"Uhhh, Dr. Hoover, it appears that this letter was addressed to you from about 2611 BC from the reign of Pharaoh Djoser, who reigned from about C2630 to C261 BC."

"O.k., o.k., so what does it say?"

"Apparently it's from Imhotep . . . ."

"You mean Lord Imhotep . . . ?"

"Uhhh, yes, Lord Imhotep . . . ."

Truth be told, I was a bit freaked out myself. Imagine getting a letter from ancient Egypt.! They had to bring in three of their best people to decipher Bob's letter. Well, it was interpreted as being a communication from Imhotep, from his era, but the contents of the letter were from Bob to me.

## XXX    XXX

"Dear Dr. Hoover, please forgive me for disappearing on you the .way I did. All I can say is simply this – I had no choice.

While I was in the room, with the acupuncture going on, Lord Imhotep himself appeared. He explained that he had 'gone to bat' for me, in a manner of speaking, concerning Senet, the woman I had fallen in love with. He explained, in no uncertain terms that he had laid out all of the groundwork, but I would have to make a decision – now or never. Now or Never. Think about that.

I think I have to say that this was the greatest, most compulsive act I had ever made in my entire life. I chose to go back into the Unknown. Lord Imhotep made it clear to me that he didn't have the power to return me to the present. I accepted his terms, his offer. And I have never regretted my decision for a moment. Well, to be honest, I may have had little pangs of homesickness or whatever, for periods of time, but no regrets.

I knew that Stella would move on with her life, after she had spent a reasonable number of months, pretending to be wracked with grief. I had mixed feelings about our son, about Anthony. To be honest, once again, I never felt very close to my son. The reason was simple – I never had the time. The truth is that he was born in the middle of a turbulent time in our lives.

Stella was involved with her career and I was involved in my career, so I guess you could say that Anthony was sort of an afterthought, a kind of orphan, you might say. We supplied him with the best, most expensive nannies we could find, and we made him understand that he was loved (in very legal terms; 'Anthony, you are loved beyond the shadow of a doubt'), but we weren't there for him. Well, what can I say? Then was then.

I have learned from Lord Imhotep that it is impossible to mourn or grieve for what might've been. Grief is <u>Now</u> and then gone. Accept that and your life will have more vibrancy, more pungency, more promise. I accept that.

But now, to go back for a bit. You might call it a 'flashback.' I went to live in Memphis, which was like Lord Imhotep's seat of power. It didn't take very long for me to realize that Lord Imhotep was considered almost a god. Or at least a connecting link to the gods. That took a little time to get used to, that my friend Imhotep was worshipped by a lot of people.

I can't really explain all of the dynamics that were in operation when I returned. All I can tell you is this; I was put to work and I went to work. I was <u>put</u> to work as a teacher, an instructor in the Arts and Sciences of the future.

'But, Lord Imhotep, my field of expertise is quite narrow, I only know something about criminal law . . . .'

'Don't worry yourself, Bab. You can concentrate on what you know best, what you know the most about. But keep in mind, your presence here constitutes the possibility of having our bright young people know what the future looks like. I think that is reason enough for you to think highly of yourself. What do you think?'

What could I think? Lord Imhotep had a way, has a way of designing ways to make the most complex things seem simple. For example, he made me understand that I was in a 'New World,' a world that would benefit from my futuristic expertise. He went so far as to establish a School of the Future for me.

I was flattered, to say the least, and a bit reluctant to be speaking to my students about the place I came from.

'Speak the truth, Bab, and you can't go wrong.' That's what he repeated to me time and time again.

'I understand what you're saying, Sir, but as an American, a Mexican-American, I can't say that I would be able to give the perspectives that an African-American, a Native-American, an Asian-American would present.'

'And no one would expect you to do that. Simply be honest and speak your truth . . . .'

'Aside from simply being an American, I don't have the experience to be able to speak for the world that I'm coming from. I know so little; only one language, only traveled to Europe on a two-week vacation, school for my criminal law degree, such a narrow gauged life.'

'Like I said, Bab, don't sweat it.'

The conversation that I'm paraphrasing allowed me to become more comfortable with my life here in Memphis. As you may very well imagine, many, many things have happened to me since I've been here. First things first. I had a very difficult time, even with Lord Imhotep's help, prying Senet away from her father, Prince Menkaure, the guy I had called 'Mr. Snakeface' when I first met him.

Prince Menkaure's biggest objection to me marrying Senet was that I wasn't a 'real person.'

'You are not a 'real person,' you came here from somewhere that I do not know or understand. Who knows? Someday you may return to wherever you came from. What will happen to my daughter if you should decide to return to the future?'

Lord Imhotep vouched for me, put the icing on the cake in a manner of speaking . . . .

'Prince Menkaure, we can all appreciate your concerns. But I must inform you that 'Bab' won't be returning anywhere. He came here on a one-way ticket. He will be here until he dies.'

And that issue was laid to rest. Prince Menkaure remained a bit crusty until Senet had our second child, a girl named Baby Senet. A boy named 'Bab' Senet Jr. (I took my wife's name because Bradford didn't sound right in Egypt). Prince Menkaure's crustiness crumbled when his two grandchildren started calling him 'Grampa! Grampa! Grampa! Grampa!' Never seen such a change happen to a middle aged man before.

Life has been rich for me, for us here. After I finally got past my fear of doing and saying the right/correct thing, I opened up what might be called 'a law firm'. Let me explain. In Egypt, during this era, a person is presumed to be guilty when accused. I didn't think that that was fair or right, so I set up this office that acts as an advocate for the accused. It's a new concept, but many people like the idea very much.

I'm sure that the future will be as rich and fantastic as the past years have been. No matter what happens we can be sure that we will all die someday. My death and the deaths/bodies of my family have been promised a place in Lord Imhotep's funeral pyramid. The honor of being in Lord Imhotep's tomb is something that I don't think the modern mentality can possibly grasp.

In any case, Doc, thank you for the excellent care you gave me and I hope this long overdue letter will find you and your family healthy, wealthy and wise.

May the Blessing of Lord Ra Shine upon you,


Always, 'Bab'


P.S. I am mailing this in Memphis, which has a badddd reputation for not delivering mail in a timely manner."


## XXX     XXX


The sun was slowly setting behind the Pacific horizon, right over there, as Jonathan finished telling me his story about Robert "Bob" Bradford, the patient who wound up in ancient Egypt. There just didn't seem to be any doubt in my mind he had spoken the truth.

"Dan, I have to tell you, I've kept this story in the shadows for a loooong time. The folks at the museum wanted me to donate Bob's letter to the museum, but I couldn't do it, I felt that I would be betraying Bob's personal story, his life, to have it put in a display case.

Unfortunately, the Director of the Egyptological Section of the museum notified the police, the police 'requested' an 'interview' concerning the communication I had received from one Robert 'Bob' Bradford, a person who had been missing for approximately twelve years.

'Uhhh, Dr. Hoover, we have been informed that you've received a letter from Robert Bradford, that you know of his whereabouts?'

I had nothing to hide, so I showed them the letter, which had been laminated, thoughtfully, by the museum people. I'll be a thousand years old before I could forget the expressions on the faces of these tough-as-nails detectives as they stared at the hieroglyphics for a few minutes before anybody said anything.

'So, these are nice drawings, Dr. Hoover, but we would like to see the letter. If you don't mind?'

'Gentlemen, that is the letter, it's written in the Egyptian language of the times . . . .'

Of course they had to bring in the Egyptian language expert, the guy who had ratted me out, to translate."

"I bet he had egg on his face."

"You better believe it. His name was Gruberhardt, never will forget him. And he was totally embarrassed to be exposed as the snitch who had told them that I had received a letter from Bob. He translated the letter very easily; after all he had read it before. After he translated it, the detectives formed a little huddle over in a far corner. Seems that they went at it, pro and con, for about twenty minutes. All I could catch from their conversation was – '2600 B.C.? B.C.?' – 'Where's the crime here?' And then '2600 What? B.C.?' 'C'mon, guys!'"

When they come back over to where I was glaring hatefully at Mr. Gruberhardt they were all handshakes, smiles, diplomatic.

'Dr. Hoover, sorry to take up your time, sir. Thank you for coming in. If we need to speak with you further about this matter, we'll give you a call.' Talk about 'cold calls.'

It didn't take a rocket scientist for them to figure out how silly and weird they would look, 'specially in the social media, if they even suggested that they were going to try to locate a missing person all the way back to ancient Egypt.

We all glared at Mr. Gruberhardt as we were escorted out of the office but I have to give it to the guy, he wouldn't give up,

'Dr. Hoover,' he whispered to me on the way down in the elevator, 'the museum would really like to have that letter; we're prepared to pay you. . . .'

'Over my dead body, Gruberhardt, over my dead body.'"

"So that's where things are today?"

"That's where things are today. Periodically I'll brose through National Geographic or one of the archeological magazines when they focus on Egypt, the pyramids, stuff like that. A couple months ago, I came across an article about Imhotep."

"Lord Imhotep, 'Bab's' buddy?"

"That's the one. Seems that they're doing some serious searching for his burial pyramid in a place called Saqqara. I hope they find it before I die, I'd love to see what the reaction will be when they find this white guy named Bob buried in the same place."

"Yeahhh, that should be very, very interesting . . . hahhahhah . . . ."

The following month, Jonathan called to tell me – "Seems that the master magician is still hiding out somewhere, the archeologists haven't come up with anything but more sand."

XXX    XXX

# CHAPTER 6

A WEEK LATER, TAKING A break from my autobio-writing, I got together with Jonathan at one of our favorite spot, the top of Signal Hill. I wanted to share one of my "most interesting stories" with him.

"You didn't tell me about this."

"I didn't have a chance; you had me enchanted with the Egyptian thing."

"Yeah, it is a pretty compelling piece of business, so what's your thing about?"

"Actually, I have two stories . . . ."

"Woww, two stories?"

"Yeah, two stories."

"Well, c'mon, let's hear 'em."

"One at a time, Dr. Hoover, one at a time."

We strolled around the gently sloped grounds of Signal Hill, enjoying the fresh Spring air, the gorgeous view of the Pacific splayed out in front of us, the buildings in downtown Los Angeles standing like a fake movie set, all kinds of people moving around us, huffing and puffing through their private exercise programs.

We sat down on one of the stone benches circling the area, just behind the low parapet that didn't block our view of the scene.

"This happened when we were young, just graduated from SoHMAA."

"Ahhh yes, when we were young. I'm glad we got past that pretty quickly."

They smiled at the idea, a common joke they shared, and gave each other high fives. A couple jogging teenagers smiled at the actions of the two old men.

"I was about six months into my practice doing what all beginners do . . . ."

"Making mistakes."

"Making mistakes and learning a lot from my mistakes too. That's one of the things that Dr. Mehta harped on – "Learn from your mistakes, learn from your mistakes.""

"How well I recall that mantra."

"That's exactly what it was too. Anyway, I had finished my last patient. I had three that day, as I recall, and I was about to pack it in when this absolutely gorgeous African-American woman strolled into my office. I wasn't making enough during my first year to afford a receptionist."

"The line forms to the left . . . ."

"She was absolutely gorgeous, Jonathan, absolutely gorgeous . . . ."

"Dan, are you going to sit here licking your chops and stroking your cat whiskers, or are you going to tell me this story that you're writing about?"

"That I've <u>written</u> about. Remember, I started writing my autobio six months before you started doing yours . . . ."

"Be that as it may – "She was absolutely gorgeous?""

"Yes, and the reason I felt that I had to stress that is because her looks are something like a central ingredient to the story."

Jonathan held back his urge to smile at his friend's way of dealing with things, details. It was one of the things that made him the great doctor he was. Daniel was never in a hurry to deal with things that demanded patience.

"O.k., so her looks are like a crucial ingredient to the story."

"Not a crucial ingredient, but a central ingredient."

"'Are you closed for the day? I didn't have the time to make an appointment . . . .' That's what she said as she entered the office.'"

"What was she? Five feet-six inches tall, skin the color of burnt cinnamon, beautifully proportioned for her size. I hate to say stuff like 36-22-36, but there it was. But it wasn't her physical stuff alone that made me feel as though an angel had entered my space."

"An angel, Daniel? An angel?"

"Yes, Jonathan, an angel. She had the appearance of someone who had been tortured, or was being tortured, but the torture had made her more beautiful, had added incredible lines to her face. She was twenty-two, I found out when I studied the chart she filled out. And the major problem she was dealing with, according to her chart, is that she felt like she was not in the right skin, that she was trying to bust out of her skin, to become somebody else.

I pressed her to give me a specific ailment, a specific area to treat. She challenged me."

'Everyone I know who talks about you, about holistic stuff, is always talking about how the whole person is taken into consideration, not just individual parts. What do you do when someone has a total body complaint?'

Like I said, she challenged me. A total body complaint, huh? I decided to work with her, using every bit of knowledge I had gained at SoHMAA. She had a good nutritional pattern going for herself. That was clear from the beginning, and she was in very good shape from exercising regularly.

"I'm the one the instructor has chosen to lead the class when she isn't there.

I decided to try to isolate her body, to treat separate sections of her body in different ways. I started with her feet and traveled up to her eyebrows, Cupping, massages, chiropractic twists and pulls, and finally acupuncture. I was really stunned to see the (therapy table) I had placed her on was drenched with perspiration after her first acupuncture session."

"Nervous reaction?"

"I assumed that to be the case. We talked about it. She admitted that she felt a bit shaky about having acupuncture the first time, that her nervousness made her perspire. That seemed to be a reasonable explanation for the first two-three sessions, but it was very puzzling when this happened every time I administered acupuncture.

Otherwise, we managed to ease her body pain somewhat. I decided to work with the idea of her being assaulted by tension, stress. I had discovered, dealing with a number of other patients, that the relief of tension, stress, anxiety, could go a long way toward alleviating physical pain."

"Ditto here. That seemed like a very simple thing to understand, but lots of us never reach that point. Go on. How many times a week? . . . ."

"I was treating her twice a week. After a month I could say that the combination of things that I was doing seemed to be working, but there was still this matter of excessive perspiration. Helene? Did I tell you that her name was Helene B. Brown?"

"No, you didn't. You described what she looked like right at the beginning, but you didn't give her a name." A sly smile creased friend Jonathan's face.

"Well, her name was Helene B. Brown. 'Helene, now that you've become aware that acupuncture doesn't hurt, what causes you to perspire so much?'"

She looked embarrassed. It took her a few beats to answer the question.

'Dr. Lane, this may sound a little off to you, but there are moments, during the acupuncture, when I feel that I'm being suffocated, that I'm being smothered. I know that that isn't happening, but that's the feeling, and it causes me to sweat like a pig.'

"What could I say to her about her feeling? I decided to continue doing what I was doing. Maybe the super sweats would stop. But there was something else happening that grabbed my attention. Helene B. Brown was physically changing . . . ."

"Physically changing?"

They paused to study the luscious forms of two young women strolling past their bench. They were almost clinical in their appraisal of the fine young bodies.

"Nice butt, but she should do something about that tire circling her waist."

"Yeah, I'd day the same thing about the blonde. So, you say she was physically changing?"

"Yes, I first noticed the voice change, she had gone from a clear soprano to a dark tenor and from there to a light baritone."

"Over what period of time?"

"We were doing acupuncture twice a week. I'd say the change really became noticeable after our sixth session. First it was the voice, then the slight wisp of a mustache appeared. Hey, what's going on here?"

"Did you ask her about the changes?"

"I didn't feel that there was any reason to, at first. But I began to suspect that her body pain and the super sweats were tied together somehow. A month, into our sessions, I felt compelled to ask – 'Ms. Brown, are you having any other medical treatments, other than the treatments you're receiving here?'"

'Yes,' she gave me a prompt answer, 'I'm receiving hormonal therapy to have a sexual reassignment.'

'You're changing from a female to a male?'

'That's correct.' I detected a defiant note in her answer. I defused the defiant attitude immediately.

'I think it's great that you should be able to have the help you need to become the person you feel you should be.'

"I could see a sigh of relief swell out of her chest. What did she think? That I was going to condemn her actions? No, none of that from a graduate of SoHMAA."

The two men exchanged high fives. No fascist, dictatorial, right-fright bigotry from them.

"It was fascinating to see, feel the changes flowing off of this young woman. As the beginning of a five o'clock shadow began to show, I noticed a certain kind of assertiveness began to happen also. She was no longer the gentle young woman who had first came into my office, she was becoming something else. . . ."

"C'mon, Dan, don't be ashamed to say it, she was becoming a man . . . ."

"Yeah, that's what happened. But there was still this matter of the steam room sweats. I made certain that it wasn't acupuncture that was the catalyst - - 'Helen?' – She changed her name, but I'll get to that later – 'Helene?' if it's not the acupuncture, then why aren't you perspiring when I do the cupping or chiropractic stuff?'

'It's really hard to explain, Dr. Lane. It's like the acupuncture, the sedative part; is that the right description for it?'"

"Good enough, go on."

'It's like the acupuncture helps me go deep into myself, deep inside of somewhere. And that's what makes me feel like I'm smothering, being suffocated. It doesn't last long, but how long _is_ long when you feel like you're being smothered?'

"Of course I couldn't answer her question, or should I say, _his_ question? Because that's what she had become in my eyes over the course of a couple-three months. I couldn't answer _his_ question, but I thought about it a lot."

"I'm feeling you, Dan, I'm feeling you, . . ."

They sat quietly for a few moments taking in the colorful display of the afternoon's sun rays on the Pacific waters.

"It came to me out of the blue, literally. Let's see what I can find out with hypnosis."

"Wowww! Hypnosis? I never would've thought of that. But, to be honest with you, I never thought of myself as being so good with hypnotic stuff."

"Well, I <u>was</u> and I <u>am</u>. So, I decided to go that route. He was a great subject, ready, willing and easily hypnotized. I felt really lucky. I don't know what I would've done if I had met great resistance, or any resistance at all.

We arranged to meet on a Friday afternoon. I was going to see how far we could go in our first hour together. That first hour morphed into a two-hour session. It took awhile for us to hit the proper groove, for me to unkink myself, and for him to relax enough to really flush the truth out.

Two hours, the first time out. I could easily say it was just a pleasant exchange, a way for us to get to know each other better. Ditto for the second session. I wasn't 'til we got into the top half of the third session that I decided to simply 'rattle the cage' a bit. I spoke very clearly and very directly – 'When you are having acupuncture, what is it that causes you to feel that you are being suffocated, smothered, that causes you to sweat so profusely?'

You should've seen the way his body stiffened, the way he made these small, desperate, squirming motions. I couldn't do anything but simply sit there and stare at this gorgeous young woman who had become a handsome young man. I thought he was having some sort of seizure. And then the drenching sweat started as he spoke."

"Jonathan, remember how you talked, wrote about how your patient, Bob's voice seemed to belong to someone else when he spoke about being in Egypt?"

"Never will forget it . . . ."

"Well, that's what happened with Helene B. Brown. I'll tell you about the name change later. It took my ears a few beats to adjust to what he was saying. It was in a heavy Southern Black dialect.

I don't want to label it a patois, like incomprehensible Jamaican village speech, or anything like that. It was English, but like English from another time. Thank God I had thought to have my state of the art recording equipment on as he spoke. It took Martha, the young woman I had hired to do the transcription, a full month to decipher and type what he had said.

Fortunately, Martha was originally from Alabama and she had an easier time of it than someone else might've had, but she was as stunned as I was by the story she heard. After the story was finally typed, I read and re-read it about four times."

'Helene, I want your permission to dramatize what came out in our session last month. That o.k. with you?'

'Dr. Lane, you've made me feel better about myself than I've ever felt, of course you can dramatize it. I trust you.'

'I appreciate that. What I had in mind was to do a radio script format, something that would be more interesting to a potential audience, if we should ever go that route, rather than a straight narrative.'

'Go for it, Dr. Lane, go for it.'

"Jonathan, tell you what. Why don't I send this over to you? I don't want to try to paraphrase any of the stories . . . ."

"That's a good idea. It's getting late too. Verona and Coco will think we've lost our compasses or something – send it – I'm dying to read it."

"You got it, buddy, you got it!"

XXX     XXX

"Jonathan, here it is, 'the sweat maker.' Let me know what you think after you've read it. As you will see, I didn't press Martha Harris, the typist, to try to deal with Helene Brown's dialect. Number one, it would've been impossible for her to do so. And if she had been capable of duplicating the word it would've made the manuscript unreadable. We've gone a lil' way into his speech pattern and that's it. Finally, after giving it a lot of thought, I decided that I would leave the narrative as is, and not try to bend it into the shape of a radio script. Or mess with it in any other kind of way. I do have inserts here and there, to give you a sense of the mood."

XXX     XXX

"I was a slave, owned by two white men. Lemme explain how that worked. My 'main master' was named Master Davis. Master Davis took advantage of how I could work with tobacco to rent me out to this tobacco factory owner. I had to pay Master Davis about $25.00 a month for allowing me the right to work.

What that meant was that I earned this money, but the factory owner gives Master Davis my pay. Master Davis then charged me for everything I got from him; what lil' food he gives me, the nasty lil' cabin I lived in, everything. I owed him pretty close to a thousand dollars. That's what he told me. And what that meant was that I always gonna be in his debt. Always.

I was twixt in between what you might call – a rock 'n a hard place. They tell me I'm about thirty-three years old now 'n I been doin' what I been doin' for a good long time. Thing is, I got a hundred 'n sixty dollars I done saved, money I done earned nickel by nickel for doin' odd jobs 'n what not. I even made a few dollars off of Master Davis. Last month he gave me two whole dollars. He musta been feeling good. Or guilty, I can't say which.

I'm thinking 'bout how I can use this money to help me escape from slavery. It's 1849, in Richmond, Virginia, and the patrollers is everywhere, things is sealed tighter than a tobacco cask for a Negro down here. Something tell me to go to see Mr. Joe Bob Smyth, he own the local store. He is a white man too, but he treat me pretty decent and he ain't got no slaves."

[Jonathan, my patient is comfortably laid out on the sofa in my office. I'm seated in my deep dish, leather covered thrift shop chair, just out of his peripheral vision. I can see the perspiration begin on his forehead. And his body begins to clench up even though he is speaking in a conversational way. It's really puzzling. Is this a three faces of Eve type thing or what?]

"Mr. Smyth, don't do nothin' but nod when I come in. He see me all the time 'cause this where I come to buy Master Davis's snuff 'n such like. He ask me what's wrong wid me, why I look so downhearted?

I tell him, my wife been sold off. He don't seem to know what to say to me. I been watching Mr. Joe Bob Smyth for a while and I've decided – this is the one what can help you. But I have to be very careful, he's still a white man. A couple people come 'n go in the store before, before I can make my plea.

I tell him, I want you to help me escape outta slavery, Mr. Joe Bob Smyth. His big blue eyes bucked like he ben shot in the boody with a twelve gauge shot gun. That's when I laid my gospel on him. I reminded him of how many times, over the years, he had talked about life, liberty and the pursuit of happiness 'n a whole bunch of other stuff.

I sorta cornered him when I asked him if he thought I was a human person, like himself. He agreed that I was a human person, like himself. So I says, why shouldn't I be a free man, just like you? I held my hat in my hands 'n looked down at the flo' just the way you 'sposed to do when you talkin' to a white man just in case somebody looked thru the sto' winder and saw us talkin' together. Virginia, 1849.

The upshot of the whole thang is that he agreed to help me escape, for half of the one hundred 'n sixty-six dollars I had accumulated. That was another booty buster for him, as a bidnessman; how in the hell could a slave get ahold of one hundred 'n sixty dollars? I had to get down into mystery about that.

Bottom line here: he agreed to help me for half of my one hundred 'n sixty dollars. I thought that that was a very gracious thang on his part. He could've asked for the whole amount and I wouldn't've had no choice but to say 'yassah.'"

[Jonathan; don't want to overpower the narrative too heavily, but please remember "Helene B. Brown," the person who is reciting something that happened, actuated by circumstances, situations, that are still beyond my understanding. And he is beginning to perspire/sweat more profusely.]

"So now, Mr. Joe Bob Smyth has agreed to do the do and he askin' me, how we gon' do this? I tell him, I don't know, suh. All I know is that I must leave heah, git outta Virginia.

We got our heads together, me 'n Mr. Smyth, and I designed the idea of me escaping in a dry goods box. He thought it was crazy, that I would wind up somewhere, starvin' to death in a box to Nowhere. I say yeah, uhh huhhh, I'd rather be dead in a box than livin' in a livin' hell on a plantation. He hesitate.

But he's got these abolitionist friends in Philadelphia. They say they will receive the box. All I got to do is get there! The time is arranged,

Halleluyah! Now, all I got to do is get there. We have agreed that I would have myself nailed into a dry goods box and shipped from Richmond to Philadelphia.

Mr. Smyth must've told me a dozen times about what it would be like being in a dry goods box for, maybe thirty hours, if everything was workin' right. I had to remind him that workin' on a plantation was worser than any box could ever be.

Awright now, so thangs is set up, I had my friend Mose, down at the carpentry shop build me a box; two feet eight inches deep, two feet wide and four feet long. It was gonna be a tight squeeze, but we had to have it like that so that it wouldn't attract too much attention.

It took about two weeks for me to put everything in place. I was nervous as a one-eyed cat peekin' thru a seafood sto' window. Had Mr. Joe Bob Smyth just took my money? If he had, there wadn't nothin' I could do about it. I couldn't take him to court 'n sue him.

If I got caught as a runaway I could have an 'R' branded on my face. Or have a foot chopped off. Or I could be given fifty or even a hundred lashes with a bull hide whip. I ben whipped by one o' them thangs and they hurts real bad. They could sell me into the deep south and I would never be able to escape. Or they could just hang me legally, for trying to escape.

All this kinda stuff was buzzin' thru my mind whilst I was goin' thru my regular twelve-fo'teen hour work day. Work. Work, work, work. All the time work, for no pay. Mose done built the box – square shaped, two feet eight inches deep, two feet wide and fo' feet deep. Mr. Joe Bob Smyth was always havin' boxes built to ship stuff here 'n there, so I didn't have to worry 'bout that being suspicious.

Come the day before March 27th, 1849, I was gonna git nailed up in the box and shipped from Richmond, Virginia to Phillydelphia, Pennsylvania. I had to think nothin' but positive. If I had let some negative stuff get up in my mind I would've went crazy.

Now here was the real problem. It had to do with not tryin' to git away too soon. If I tried to get away too soon, it would give Master Davis 'n nim too much time to try to track me down. I managed to git off work in the tobacco factory by injuring both my hands. Mr. Hynes, the factory owner was fit to be tied. But there was nothin' he could do about my havin' two hands that was so badly injured I couldn't do my work.

He sent me home to the plantation with a note, tellin' Master Davis that he was gonna lose a day of my pay because I had ben dumb enough to get myself injured. I could read a lil' bit. Master Davis was gonna lose a day of my pay. Master Davis was gonna lose a day of <u>my</u> pay. That made me mad as hell.

So, here I am, walkin' down the street, hands hurtin', on my way to the plantation, mind on nothin' but Freedom. And who should I run into but a couple of the local white trash boys? Always lots o' them hangin' 'round, usually half drunk. They stop me 'cause they want to, just to be devilish.

They wanna play with me. I got to go 'long with the game else my escape plan is knocked away. I do what they want me to do: I do a lil' dancin', 'some buck 'n nigga stuff' they calls it. One of 'em notices my messed up hands 'n asks me 'bout that. I tell 'im Master Davis stomped on my hands for not waitin' on him proper. That's when they backed off 'cause they know who Master Davis is, and if they found out that they was messin' 'round wid one o' Master Davis top niggas, a couple white trash types, they would be in heap big trouble.

When they got the information that I was one of Master Davis' top niggas, they give me a couple kicks in the booty and that was that. I made a quick, roundabout detour to Mister Joe Bob Smyth's back door, a bit tired from doin' 'some buck 'n nigga stuff.'"

[Jonathan, I have to tell you, I had basically written my waterlogged, sweat stained sofa off. But it didn't matter, I was beginning to feel what an enslaved human felt like, one who was willing to die, trying to escape in a dry goods box, rather than be worked to death.]

"Mister Joe Bob Smyth hadn't turned me in, hadn't messed wid me in my way. He was Righteous. He bound my hands with poultices of flax meal and gave me a place to sleep in his storeroom. He had made arrangements for these boxes of dry goods, one of 'em <u>being me</u>, to be picked up at 4 am. I went back there in his storeroom, hands hurtin' on fire, 'n laid down on some sacks, eyes wide open. I was gonna save my sleepin' for freedom."

[Jonathan, stay with the narrative. Helene had to dismount the sweat soaked sofa, to go take a pee. I had a chance to take a breather. I felt like I had been holding my breath. She's back, here we are, here we go.]

"I laid up there thinkin' 'bout what Master Davis was gon' say when he found out I was gone. I could just see 'im in his big ol' house, cussin' 'n fussin', sayin' nasty thangs about me, about that Tubman woman, runnin' back 'n forth, stealin' folks property away, about the Underground railroads, po' white trash tryin' to buy they way into polite society. All kinds o' stuff.

Yeah, Master Davis had some bones to pick with damned near everybody. His favorite thing was sayin', 'these niggas oughta be grateful that we pulled 'em 'way from heathenism 'n taught 'em how to do an honest day's work.'

Well, ain't too much I could think about what he said 'bout an honest day's work. An honest day's work 'sposed to give you some payment. That's what the white folks expect 'n that's what they get. But not us, not the po' Black people in slavery."

[Everything suddenly went on Pause. Helene stopped talking and laid there for a full two minutes, dead as a nail. I didn't know whether I should call 911 or what. Instinct kicked in. I remembered my hypnotic cues. I asked – "and then what happened?" The perspiration was like a narrow gauge lava flow, from his brow, his chest, all of the visible areas.]

"I was being loaded onto a horse driven wagon, to be taken to the rail station and from there to the freight ship takin' us 'cross the Potomac. From there I would be carted to the train to Phillydelphia. I had packed enough tobacco casks to know how stuff was sent. I had a bladder of water and a few biscuits to see me thru.

Now, here I am, in this box, cramped into a sittin' position, with just enough room for me to move my arms a bit and shift my body a bit, but it was real tiresome. Real tiresome. From Mr. Smyth's store to the Express office was a mile. It's a mile I'll never forget as long as I live.

Goin' that terrible mile, stuffed in that box, I had a chance to go back thru everything that had ever happened to me. Most of what came to my mind was pretty ugly; not knowin' who my Momma 'n Daddy was because we had been sold off to different folks. That hurt me a lot.

I thought about being whipped out to work before the sun came up, barely havin' enough to eat and hardly enough clothes to cover my body, even in the winter time. Work, all the time, work. I was a field hand under an overseer who was so mean 'n evil he used to bullwhip people's eyes out of they heads. He was a devil with that bullwhip!

They said that none of the field hand had ever lived longer than five years on this man's plantation. I was in my fourth year when he died. Some say that Delcine the cook poisoned his food. I can't rightfully say what happened. All I know is that I was sold off. Master Davis found out that I know a lot about tobacco, so he hired me out to work for Master Allen in his tobacco factory.

Master Davis probably saved my life. I don't think I could've lasted too much longer out there in the fields. Yeah, he probably saved my life, but I couldn't be too grateful 'cause I was still a slave. A whole bunch of thangs went thru my mind travelin' that mile to the Express Office.

I prayed to Almighty God for salvation. I prayed that He should not let me get caught and taken back into slavery. I tried to see what freedom would look like in my mind, but it was too dark.

They unloaded me from the wagon and toted me onto the station dock. I heard a couple heavy thumps on my box and I knew the clerk had stamped where the box was going. I knew that from that was the way they stamped tobacco casks. My heart was so far up in my throat I couldn't hardly swallow.

After a while, seemed like hours, somebody come along, lifted my box up and tipped me into a baggage car, upside down. I was on my head. After a few minutes being on my head. I felt my eyes about to pop out and the blood fillin' up in the veins in my temples made my head feel like it was about to explode.

My whole body went into a cold sweat and I just know I was gonna die. I just know it, that was the feelin' I had.

As the train started steamin' up to go, I prayed with all my might that I would be saved from the torture of stayin' on my head."

[Jonathan, remember, two foot eight inches deep, two feet wide and four feet long. As a semi-claustrophobic I almost had a panic attack just listening to this story.]

"Halleluyah! The good Lord answered my prayers. Somebody pushin' 'n movin' stuff around, in order to make room for other boxes, laid me over on my side. It took a lil' while for my blood to get right again, for the veins in my head to settle down, but after a while I felt like myself again.

I was alright for a while 'cause I just decided to stop tryin' to think about anything, just bumpin' along with all the rest of the boxes 'n crates – 'til this dull ache started up 'n down my right side, the side I was layin' on. I could shift my weight off my shoulder joint to get some pressure off, but mostly I had a heavy, dull, hurtful feelin'.

The heat in the box was really bad and my clothes was soakin' wet from sweat."

[It was easy to connect the dots now. I was mopping perspiration off my brow.

"From time to time I would close my eyes and try to think of a good time I once had, or somethin' like that. I couldn't do it, I couldn't think of anything good that ever happened to me. I thought strong on my wife, Maylene, and that made me cry a lil' bit.

Mostly I remembered how Master Davis used to come down to our shack whenever he wanted to, make me get out, and have his way with my wife, with Maylene. He must've told me more than a dozen times, 'that's a mighty fine lil' woman you got there, Henry mighty fine.'

Master Davis was the main reason why we didn't have no children. Every time Maylene thought she was in a family way she would go see Sister Woman, to get some kinda herbs or somethin' that would cause her to abort. She told me that she wouldn't be runnin' the risk of havin' no slave master's baby.

Come to think of it, out of the twenty-six women on the plantation about twenty of 'em had children by Master Davis. That man was a dirty dog. He even had sex with some of the daughters he had by the women on the plantation.

I felt real bad about Maylene. I found out that he had sold her down south because she was doin' the abortions. He couldn't stand that. She was causin' him to lose field hands, mo' slaves. I don't know how he found out, I guess somebody just couldn't keep they mouth shut.

I thought I was dead at one point. It just didn't seem like I could be alive, hardly able to move my body, every muscle stiff from being locked in place. I clenched my teeth together and tightened my messed up hands into fists and prayed. I prayed to God to give me the strength to hold out, to keep my mind together and not crack.

It was like being in a hole somewhere. The box had become a part of my skin and I wanted to pull my skin off but I couldn't do that 'cause my skin was the box. I became confused for a time.

Had I been in the box a day, or two days? Was I goin' in the right directions? What would happen to me if the box was goin' South instead of North? What if somebody had made a mistake? Was I goin' crazy?

I could see myself in a baggage room somewhere, slowly starvin' to death 'cause I had made a vow on my soul's damnation that I would rather be dead than be a slave again."

XXX    XXX

# CHAPTER 7

[I SNAPPED HELENE BACK TO the present and he laid in place, blinking for a few seconds, like the light was too bright for him.

"Helene, we're going to end this session for today, we'll continue tomorrow, same time."

"Whatever you say, doc, whatever you say."

I think he could've carried on, to be honest about it. I was calling a break because I couldn't take anymore. I had gone through enough for one day.]

Next day . . . .

"The train was steamin' to a stop, I could tell from the way my crate was bumped back and forth. After a while somebody slammed the freight train doors open and I could hear voices and smell river water. We had reached the Potomac. I was sure of it, which meant that I was headed in the right direction, at least. My spirits picked up a lil' bit. I was beginning to feel like I had a real chance to make it.

The next thing I know I had been carted onto a boat (I could feel the waves) and turned up on my head again! I peed on myself when I just broke down 'n cried. I couldn't help myself. I'll never forget the feelin' of tears runnin' down my forehead upside down.

Lord have mercy, Jesus! I prayed. The motion of the boat, bouncin' me back and forth, rubbed the top of my head raw and gave me a fearsome headache. I don't know how long I was in that position. It could've been an hour or a day. I couldn't tell which.

The bouncin' caused me to be sick sick sick and I came close to drownin' in my own bile. Once again I prayed for the strength to carry on, to be saved and, once again, my prayers was answered. A couple sailors, looking for a place to loaf 'n play some cards, came into the place where my box was.

This is the way they was talkin' . . . .

'I got the cards, you bring all the money you wanna lose?'

'Hah, that's what I like, a born loser who likes to put up a big front.'

'Well, you know what the ol' sayin' is, nothin' is cheaper than talk. I'll let my Kings 'n Queens speak for me. Here, help me lay this crate on the side.'

It took all of my will power to keep myself from screamin' when they slammed me, when they slammed my box onto the side. I thanked the Lord and the two sailors for takin' me off my head. But somehow, when they sat on the box, it seemed like I could feel the weight of their bodies on the box. I could hardly breathe from the excitement of knowin' that the slightest noise would give me away.

The sailors played a lively game of cards, slammin' they cards onto the box, drummin' they heels up 'gainst the box 'n all, talkin' all the time.

'There, take that! So talk is cheap! I think my Ace, King and Jack O'hearts beats your hand, face up!'

'Awwww, just pure luck . . . ."

'If that's all it takes to beat you, buddy, I'm satisfied.'

"Durin' the time they was sittin' on my box, playin' they card game, a fly got inside my box through one of the tiny holes Mose had made for me to breathe thru. It must've been one o' them stingin' river flies 'cause it caused me a heep o' pure misery. Everywhere it crawled it stung me. It lit on my nose, walked up the middle of my nose to my forehead and back to the tip of my nose again, stingin' all the way. It crawled across my left eyelid, my right eyelid, my lips, in and out of my right ear.

I was tortured somethin' awful by that fly and wasn't nothin' I could do about it. I was afraid to try to squash it for fear that I would make a noise and be discovered. Finally, the sailors decided to go back to work.

Real strange thing happened. The minute the sailors left, that fly left too. I don't know where it went but I was very happy that it went wherever it went. I had to thank the sailors for takin' me off my head and placin' me on my side. But being in that position grew pretty tiresome too, after a lil' while.

I have to say prayer, hope, and the belief that my journey would have to come to an end, sooner than later, one way or another, kept me alive. Then, as though some miracle had happened I heard somebody call it – "That's Washington!"

"I was unloaded with all the other freight and placed on a horse-wagon, right side up – Thank God! Bumpin' long in the wagon to the train depot I passed a section where I could smell greens, beans, side meat, candied yams, hush puppies and bar-be-que. The smells made my mouth water somethin' fierce. I managed to fumble a couple saggy biscuits in my mouth and drink a lil' out of my bladder.

Washington seem to be hotter than any place I had been in my box so far. Long, long ride to the train depot. I could tell we had reached the depot from hearin' the steam engines hiss and all these railroad noises.

After a long while, some men jumped up on the wagon and started unloadin' the crates, includin' my box. The way I figured it, I had two more times to be unloaded, this time and when we got to Philly-delphia. I felt like a wet dish rag."

[Call it sympathetic bonding, or whatever, but I had definitely developed a sweat level that was never a part of my personality make up . . . .]

"Two men discussed whether or not they should send the box, my box, labeled 'Express,' or not. A Bossman came along and said – 'Dammit! It's labeled 'Express' and that's how it's gonna go. And it says – 'This side up' – so, move it gentlemen!'

And that's the way I wound up in the baggage car 'This side up.' By this time I was halfway out of my senses most of the time. I felt like beatin' my fists up 'sides the walls of the box to scream for somebody to get me out but I was feelin' too weak. And besides, nobody would've heard me in the baggage car anyway.

It was like I was havin' strange dreams and I wasn't even asleep. One minute I would be on a giant swing, floatin' back 'n forth like some kind of giant butterfly, and a few minutes later, my body would feel like a heavy stone sinkin' down into the middle of a deep, black river. In some strange way I could feel the weight of the boxes and crates stacked on top of me and under me.

I wanted to go out of myself but there was nowhere to go. In addition to everything else, there was another box blockin' the air holes in my box and it was becomin' more and more hard to breath. I worked on my head, doin' different things; I made myself count up to one hundred, which was the biggest number I knew. Then I said my ABCs over and over. Sometimes I couldn't get no farther than F or R and then I'd have to start off again because I couldn't keep my mind straight.

That worried me a lot, losin' my mind in that box. I didn't want to go crazy in a box. I broke down and cried again when I felt the train pullin' up to a stop. I really can't say why I was cryin', or what I was cryin' about. It just didn't seem right to me at all. Why should I spend my life in a box when all of the rest of the world was walkin' 'round free as birds?

Tears for every day of a life that I had been a slave, forced to work like a mule for the white folks. I cried thinkin' about how bad they had treated me. I was still cryin' when they started unloadin' the freight train. Philly-delphia!

I had made it. But I still had to be careful 'cause I could be discovered and taken straight back to Virginia. I had heard about some cases like that. Slave catchers was always hangin' 'round train depots.

My box was unloaded and stacked with the rest of the freight. There was a lot of bouncin' 'n pushin' 'n bumpin' around. I prayed that they wouldn't stack me up on my head again. After a while everything went quiet. Now I started thinkin' – would the man who was supposed to claim the box come? What if we had some kind of mix up on the date and the time?

A hundred doubts played on my mind. Maybe I would just stay where I was 'til I died. Seems like I had been thinkin' these kinds of thoughts for a loonng time before I felt my box being moved, loaded on a dolly. A man with an Irish voice was there to claim me.

He said – 'I'm here to pick up a box from J.B. Smyth, Richmond, Virginia, for Dr. Jim McKim. Here's the invoice.'

Once again I was loaded on a horse wagon, right side up, and hauled away. The man with the Irish voice didn't seem to be in too much of a hurry. He even stopped to have a drink at a saloon, I could tell from hearin' the men cussin' in carryin' on. I was so excited I felt like my heart was gonna pinch a hole thru my chest. Finally, he took me to where he was 'sposed to deliver me. He said – 'That is heavy box, Dr. McKim, I wanna tell ya, sur.'

'I'm sure it is, Dan, here's a little extra for your effort.'

'Thank ya, sur, thank ya.'

That's what they said to each other, then it was real quiet for a few minutes after I heard a door closed. Then it was like a whole bunch of people started talkin' at the same time.

'Somebody get a crowbar!'

'Knock on the box, see if he's still alive.'

'Are you alive inside there?'

It took me a bit to find my voice. It was like I had forgot how to speak.

'Yessuh, I'm alive." These was white voices, I had to say 'yessuh.'

A few minutes later they had knocked the cover off my box and helped me out of the box. I was weak as a new born baby, but I was free. They gave me some water and told me who they was – Dr. Jim McKim, Professor C.P. Cleveland, Mister Lewis Thompson and Mr. William Still.

After I told them what my name was – Henry Brown, Dr. McKim said – 'that <u>was</u> your name, your new name is <u>Mr.</u> Henry 'Box' Brown.'"

Helene B. Brown looked dazed when I snapped her back to the present. He sat up slowly and stared at me. I was crying, I couldn't hold back the tears.

Dr. Hoover, my name is Henry 'Box' Brown, that's what that 'B' stands for, and if it isn't, it will be as soon as I can get to City Hall."

XXX   XXX

"I got permission from Daniel to allow Verona to read Helene B. Brown/a.k.a. Henry 'Box' Brown's story."

"No problem. I've already given CoCo the opportunity to read it. Sure, let her read it."

I didn't give Verona a big fat explanation of the transcript/manuscript, I just laid it on her desk and said, "read this when you have time."

A couple days later she handed it back to me. She had a glazed look in her eyes. She didn't say anything; she just strolled out onto the back veranda and sat there. I let her sit out there by herself for a solid hour. After you've been married for a while, you get a feeling for when your partner needs to be left alone, or whatever you know when they need to be allowed to have their private space.

I joined her after an hour or so. Beautiful summer day, the garden was in full bloom, the sunset making gorgeous colors on the sky palette as it slowly settled below the horizon. We linked our hands together, she leaned her head on my shoulder.

"It's hard for me to imagine how cruel slavery was, but now I have some idea of how it drove some people to do incredible things to be free."

Verona Obregon-Hoover, the hard bitten criminal prosecutor spoke in the saddest tones I had ever heard. Verona Obregon-Hoover, this cool one, cried on my shoulder. There was nothing I could think to say, to ease the blues she felt, I was feeling her.

## XXX XXX

Sunday morning on the Hill again, Dr. Daniel Lane II and Dr. Jonathan Hoover strolled the perimeter of the park, settled onto their favorite stone bench overlooking the city, extending out to the beautiful blue Pacific.

"Yeah, that was pretty much the reaction I got from CoCo when she read the copy. You would think that someone who dealt with mentally ill people all day would be, would have a harder shell on their feelings than most other people. CoCo cried about what she had read. I didn't see her cry, but I could tell."

They were silent for a few minutes, comfortable with each other. "Dan, I think we're fortunate men to be married to women who have that depth of feeling." Daniel Lane nodded in agreement.

"The transcript ends with Helene a.k.a. Henry running off to City Hall to have a name change. That the end of the story? Did you ever see her, uhhh, him after that?"

"O my God yes! He was in and out of my office a number of times over the course of the next couple years. Seems he had become a pretty good amateur soccer player and he was always coming to me for acupuncture with his various aches and pains."

"Tell me about it, I have a bad knee from my days playing 'the beautiful game' against a bunch of wild Brazilians."

"Guaranteed aches and pains. Well, anyway, I treated him, but the Biggie came about during the second year of his soccer playing days. He came into my office at the appointed time, a huge smile on his handsome face. 'Helene' had fully transitioned into a guy named Henry Box Brown II.

He had really staked a legitimate claim on the name. Here's how he ran it down to me."

'I started thinking a lot about my name, my new name, and where I was born . . . Philadelphia. It was like I had a hole suddenly drilled into my consciousness. I reached out to the Alex Haley DNA Foundation. These people do marvelous work about African-American genealogy. They have branches in Los Angeles, New York, and a few places in between.

I explained to Dr. Ralph Vernon what my feelings were, what my suspicions were, what I wanted to be definitely established. 'No problem, brother, no problem. That's why we're here.'

I went to the Los Angeles branch of the organization and had blood tests and mouth swabs done. I thought I was related to the man, Henry 'Box' Brown, and I wanted to have that validated or disproved. I wanted to know who I was, in relation to him. It took a week, one solid week, for Dr. Vernon to pull me back into his office. I should've been on my guard against Dr. Vernon's quirky sense of humor; as an example, he suggested, early on, that I might be a descendant of one of the generals in Hannibal's army.

I told him that I couldn't relate to that, emotionally. Then he explained that he was talking about that great half back who had played for the Pittsburgh Steelers, and the fans who had labeled themselves 'Hannibal's Army.' Or whatever they called themselves back then. (Franco Harris.)

He finally got serious and explained to me in clear bright terms – 'Helene'/ Henry, here's the deal. We managed to contact a historical organization that had shards of Henry 'Box's' original box and some of his sweat stained clothes. Our DNA testing establishes that you are, indeed, a relative of the late Henry 'Box' Brown.

Now, what we're working to do is establish the exact extent of that relationship. We'll get back to you.

They got back to me a week later. I was a direct descendant of Mr. Henry 'Box' Brown. It would take ten minutes to explain to who was who and how that who was related to that other who. But the bottom line showed that I was a direct descendant of <u>Mister</u> Henry <u>Box</u> Brown. I felt like I was floating for a whole day after I got that information. I could righteously lay claim to being a direct descendant of one of the most courageous men in American history. He came out of a box and I followed him.'

"That wasn't the only confidential information he shared with me."

'Dr. Hoover, I'm going to Copenhagen, Denmark, next week . . . .'

'Vacation?'

'No sir, I'm going to have myself 'fully established,' you might say, as a man.'

I had to admit to him that I couldn't quite understand what he was talking about.

'Well, Doc, it seems that there's a hermaphroditic element involved with my transition.'

"Huh? Hermaphrodite? Did I hear hermaphrodite?"

"That's what you heard, my friend. I was just as surprised as you are. He wanted to make absolutely certain that he would be a complete man. As you know, dating back to the Christine Jorgensen days, the Danes have a great reputation for 'improving' transsexual/transgender assignments.

So, he goes to Copenhagen, Denmark . . . ."

Both of their heads were turned by the sight of two young women, both buffed up and blonde, punching and jabbing at each other, twenty – thirty yards away, on the southern slope of the Hill. The blondes were obviously seasoned professionals, they could tell from the way they bobbed and weaved, counter punched without landing blows, picked off each other's jabs with flicks of their light gloved fists. Always something interesting happening on the Hill.

"He went to Denmark? . . ."

"Right, he went to Denmark and returned, absolutely glowing with good vibes. 'Doc, everything is cool with me now, you know, you know what I'm saying?'

I had to confess that I wasn't exactly certain if I knew what he was saying or not. He made what he was saying a bit clearer."

'The physical elements of the female part of me were left in Denmark. Right now I'm as much male as any male. Wanna see?'

"Caught ya by the short hairs, huh? Jonathan?"

"If you wanted to put it that way. I had to tell him that there was no need for him to show me anything, I took his word for the Gospel truth."

"Talk about a Journey of Discovery?! I'll take a Helene B. Brown, later known as Henry Box Brown II story over anything they're currently showing in the local theatres."

"And there's more, the story doesn't end on the transition."

"Really? There's more?"

"There's more. Henry met a lovely Ethiopian woman in Copenhagen. Zola Wole MaKonnen was majoring in Sociology at the University of Copenhagen; she was a great grandniece of the last royal family in Ethiopia, Emperor Haile Selassie and all of that . . . . ."

"Wowww!"

"They fell in love and when the course of events got to me they were at stage three of their wedding preparations. 'Doctor Hoover, I would like for you to be my best man.'"

'It's a done deal, Henry. What do I have to do? When is it? And where?'"

XXX     XXX

# CHAPTER 8

"It was one of those balmy evenings that only seem to happen in Southern California, Laguna Beach, California. I was invited to be one of three hundred carefully screened guests at the Henry Box Brown-Zola Wole MaKonnen's wedding.

'We were sworn to secrecy about the event.' We felt compelled to do it like this, Doc, to keep things from becoming a tabloid/media/circus event. You know the kind of junk they write about? – 'Transgender-cross dresser – a.k.a. Henry Box Brown marries Ethiopian-princess-lion-tamer' – or some such crap.'

I totally agreed with him and I've never spoken about the event 'til now. However, I'm pretty sure that CoCo told Verona about it, years ago."

"Some people know how to keep a secret. Go on . . . ."

"Like I said, it was a gorgeous Spring evening, temperature about the same as your body temp. Chairs arranged on the beach, a collection of really colorful characters. I feel that I have to say – 'characters' – because each of them seemed so distinct. No body made from a cookie cutter in the mix.

I don't want to overstate this, but there were such a harmonious blend of elements that I actually had the feeling that I was present at some sort of sacred ritual . . . ."

"Maybe that's what a wedding is supposed to feel like."

"Well, as you know, Laguna has a certain kind of charm of its own about it, and charm doesn't come close to describing what the real vibe is like. A setting sun, the ocean rolling in like a soft blue carpet, gentle breezes with the slight tang of the sea spilling in on us. . . ."

"My goodness, Doctor Lane, you sound like some kind of poet."

"Jonathan, take my word, it was the kind of scene that would've forced you to see it in a poetic way. From the beginning, when the priest sounded his first notes on the conch shell, to the conclusion of the ceremony with a kiss that sealed the deal, there was magic in all of it.

After the wedding, when people trooped up the cliff to enjoy the wonderful food and drinks at the post wedding reception, I took a lil' stroll on the beach. CoCo waved me and joined the people at the cliff side celebration.

There was something the priest had said several times about ancestors. I can't recall the exact words now, but it had something to do with how much our ancestors had to do with who we are. That really struck a chord with me, considering what I knew about Henry Box Brown II, formerly known as Helene B. Brown.

'Henry,' I asked him one day while I was giving him a chiropractic procedure for a jammed neck, 'when you were Helene, what was the 'B' for?'

He laughed. 'Actually it didn't stand for anything, I just wanted to have a letter between Helene and Brown.'"

"Hahhahhah. I like that. So, they got married and lived happily ever after. Where are they now incidentally?"

"They've been living in Denmark since their marriage."

"These weren't people who let a lot of grass grow under their feet."

"You got that right. The interesting thing, to me, is how they wound up in Copenhagen. Zola's family had immigrated to Denmark after the communist takeover/revolution. I never found out why they had picked Denmark 'cause it wasn't my business. But, evidently the MaKonnens had escaped from Ethiopia with a substantial amount of money stashed in a couple Swiss bank accounts.

Henry had married into a wealthy expatriate family and I can tell you this, they adored him, you could tell from the way they smiled and learned throughout the whole wedding ceremony.

So, why Denmark after the wedding? This is the way Henry put it to me.

'Zola and I decided that we didn't want to live in a country where a man like that could be considered, thought of as being fit to be the president of one of the greatest countries this world has ever known. No matter whether he won or lost, the simple fact that so many thought that he was qualified to be the president; that was enough for us.

Zola had family in Copenhagen and I had grown to love the Danes; a kind of quirky blend of fun loving, freewheeling, beer drinking, very rational, progressive thinking individuals, so why not Denmark? Aside from the excellent health care system that had treated me so well. Some of our friends argued against the move.'

'Ahhh, c'mon, Henry-Zola, be sensible. Even if this creep won it would only be for one term, I think that one term would be enough to force people to see the error that they'd made.'"

"Phil, you can't make book on that, look at how far Bush drove the country over into a ditch during <u>Cheney's</u> <u>term</u> <u>in</u> <u>office</u>, look at the price we're still paying for the madness in Baghdad and Afghanistan. Sorry pal, this is one debacle I want to look at from a distance."

"I even put in my two cents. 'Look, I don't have to remind you guys that Europe, including Denmark, has been attacked by terrorists . . . .'

They laughed in my face. 'And just what do you think that that fascistic-pathological lying egomaniac is? Terrorism can be defined in lots of ways, Dr. Lane. Lots of ways.'

So, off they went. Zola Wole MaKonnen got her degree in Sociology from Copenhagen U. and joined the faculty of Copenhagen U. Henry got a bug in his butt and went for a degree in Psychology. He specializes in counseling for transgender people."

"Wowwww! Now that really goes to show you that truth is stronger than fiction . . . ."

"Sorry, Jonathan, that's not the end of the story . . . ."

"There couldn't be more, you're just making stuff up!"

"Cross my heart 'n hope to cry, there's more."

"Let's hear it."

"Once again, this is what they told us when they came to visit last year. As you know, they're mounting a strong lobbying effort to have a Henry 'Box' Brown Day in America . . . ."

"Yeahhh, I've read a couple articles about that."

"So far, so good, but there's lot more work to be done. Anyway, while they were here they talked about what it felt like to be day time television stars in Denmark . . . ."

"You're making this up. Stop!"

"Nope, it's the buck naked truth. This is the way it happened. They were sitting in their local coffee house one Saturday morning, doing the kind of thing that people do in Denmark, when this television producer came over. He explained that he was producing a television series called 'Copenhagen Today' and he thought that they would be the ideal couple to host one segment of the show.

They thought it would be a kick, so they took him up on it. The producer wanted the show to reflect more diversity and who would reflect that better than two nut brown people? A woman from Ethiopia and an African-American. Their 'job' is just to take their audiences around Copenhagen, and the surrounding areas, eating, drinking, having a good time. They're also gotten roles in a few other television shows, as a spinoff from 'Copenhagen Today

"Well, I'll be dammed!"

"Hahh hahhah, that's what I said too. Hey, what time are we meeting CoCo and Verona at the Ichiban House?"

"We told 'em 1:30, we're fifteen minutes late."

"Well, let's go, you know how hungry those ladies are for Ichiban's sushi after they've shopped all our money away."

They exchanged high fives, pleased to share the vibes of an old joke.

"Ohhh, Dan, by the way, you said you had two stories you wanted to tell me. What's the second one?"

"It'll have to wait 'til after lunch, Jonathan. I'm too weak from hunger to get into it now."

"That's right, play the suspense card on me, huh?"

They walked briskly to their cars, looking forward to having a lunch date with their wives.

### XXX    XXX

The Ichiban House Japanese Restaurant. The two men were welcomed by a smiling, graciously bowing hostess . . . "Please be welcomed to Ichiban House Japanese Restaurant, please to follow me, please . . . ."

Jonathan and Daniel exchanged coded eye glances. Same ol' Ichiban. The ambience of the place put them in a smiling mood the minute the door was opened for them. Their hostess led them to where their wives were pretending to be waiting impatiently.

"Well, it's about time!" Verona held her wrist watch up and pushed her bottom lip out in a playful pout.

"Ladies, please don't be angry, we were caught in a traffic jam." CoCo shook her head with fake disgust.

"Daniel, you are such a terrible liar! Signal Hill is only four blocks from here and the restaurant is on the east side of the street, same as the restaurant, how could you get caught in a traffic jam?"

Jonathan defused the whole situation by suavely slipping in obliquely.

"Now that we've gotten all of that out of the way, how about a couple bottles of Ichiban for two thirsty husbands?"

They shared smiles all around. Jonathan, had done his diplomatic work without effort, accompanied by an elfin expression. CoCo patted the seat beside her. Verona accepted a peace making peck on her nose. The hostess was replaced by a smiling waitress, waiting patiently to be noticed.

"Uhhh, Daniel, how about a chilled Ichiban?"

"Jonathan, you must be a mind reader . . . ."

"The men will have two beers and we will have two cups of Oolong tea.

The groove was happening. Daniel and Jonathan, ordinarily non-beer drinking guys, loved having chilled bottles of Ichiban when they came to the restaurant.

"It goes so well with the food."

"That's the way we feel about the tea."

The pattern was established. The men had a couple bottles of Ichiban each, and the women became designated drivers automatically. It never took longer than five minutes for their drinks to be placed in front of them.

Daniel kicked it off with one of his favorite toasts.

"Here's looking at you, kids . . . may the road to Hell grow green awaiting your arrival."

They smiled, sipping their drinks, and studied the design of the restaurant as they always did. It was a loosely patterned Japanese village: an open kitchen lining the north wall, alive with a collection of briskly moving chefs, expertly dicing and slicing, frying and broiling. Comfortable dining booths on the east and south walls – one step down into a central dining area lined with tables and chairs.

The effect was almost theatrical. They were into their second year of enjoying superb Japanese cuisine and the atmosphere. And the waitresses liked them because they were light-hearted, fun to serve and left generous tips.

"How did we discover this place?"

The question surfaced periodically, whenever anyone in the quartet wanted to egg Verona into repeating the well-worn story of how they came to regard the Ichiban as their favorite restaurant.

"Well, as I'm sure you can all remember, my girlfriend, Shirley Yamaguchi, down at the Department of Justice, came to my desk one afternoon with this beautiful little magazine called, 'Japan Today.'"

"Verona, you want to read a magazine about Lil' Tokyo, Japan town, where to go? Stuff like that."

"Sure, leave it, I'll read it on my lunch hour."

"Let me know what you think about this magazine, especially about the Norisato restaurant review article."

"Maybe I should've had some suspicions about Shirley's motive for recommending the Norisato article, she was a well-known practical joker, but I was so bogged down in legal briefs I passed over her possible motive. O.k., I'm on my lunch 'hour.' Which meant thirty-two minutes, a tuna fish panini and a bottle of Spring water.

"Japan Today." Lovely photographs, lots of info about the who, what, where and how of Lil' Tokyo, a well put together piece of "come and see."

Mrs. Jane Narisato's review of Ichiban forced me to read it twice. Maybe three times. It made me smile a lot, but it also left me feeling extremely puzzled.

[Mrs. Jane Narisato restaurant review:

"One has to wonder about the way to get to the restaurant affectionately entitled Ichiban. Ichiban's large window beckoned us to come through. There were six of us, all totally inflamed of what we heard about this establishment entitled 'Ichiban.'

We were strongly welcomed by the husband and wife of Ichiban, Mr. and Mrs. George Matsumoto. We were soon at our reserved table, safely involved with our Kaiseki style dining. Kaiseki, to the Unaware, is a way of doing food that balances taste, texture, appearance and colors of the food.

Dishes are delicately arranged, often with real leaves and flowers, as well as garnishes meant to resemble natural plants and animals. How can I describe the delicate emotion of the flavors we tasted? Let me try.

A long time ago Kaiseki would be a bowl of miso soup and three side dishes. Now Kaiseki included the appetizer, sashimi, a simmered dish, grilled dish and a steamed dish. The chef can add others. Here is what we had, including my husband, Mr. Fred Narisato;

1) Sakizuke = appetizer
2) Hassun = 2nd course. One kind of sushi and some small side dishes
3) Mukozuke = a sliced dish of sashimi
4) Takiawase = vegetables served with meat, fish, tofu. The ingredients were simmered separate.
5) Futamono = soup
6) Yakimono = grilled fish
7) Su-zakana = vegetables in vinegar. This to clean the palate.
8) Shiizakana = a hot pot. Mmmmm . . .
9) Gohan = a rice dish made with good things
10) Ko no mono = pickled vegetables.
11) Tome-wan = vegetable soup served with rice
12) Mizumono = ice cream! Fruit! Cake! Desert!

Did I mention that there was also tea, beer and sake? All of us where chosen to drink a good deal of sake. I had enough of my share. My friends, including my husband, Mr. Fred Narisato, also had their shares of sake.

In Kyoto, Kaiseki-style cooking is sometimes known as Kyoto cooking. And it can be expensive. Yes, expensive. One pays $125.00 to $340.00 without drinks. One can have the cheaper lunch/$34.00 to $68.00 or even down to bento/$17.00 to $34.00.

The Ichiban Japanese Restaurant must rank Number One on my book and it will be so with you also, if you visit soon. At the end of the day I can only say this – dining at the Ichiban was a subliminal experience for Mr. Fred Narisato, my husband, and the friends who come with us. Hopefully you will enjoy also."

Later that day Shirley peeked into my office.

"Verona, you had a chance to check out 'Japan Today?'

What could I say? No reason to lie about it.

"Uhhh, yeah, Shirley, I read it on my lunch hour. Really great photography . . . ."

"So, what did you think of Mrs. Narisato's restaurant review?"

She had me by the short hairs. I was tempted to try to b.s. my way past her question, but something warned me, don't try to b.s. Shirley, she's basically b.s. proof.

"Well, to be absolutely honest with you, I have to say that I've never read a restaurant review . . . uhhh . . . quite as interesting as this one."

"Interesting?" Shirley prodded me a bit, smiling slyly.

"Uhhh, yes, I would say . . . interesting."

Shirley almost fell across my desk, laughing so hard tears came to her eyes. It took her a few minutes to collect herself, to tell me what was funny.

"Verona, to say that Mrs. Narisato's restaurant review is 'interesting' is the understatement of the year." She went on to explain – "there are many people in Lil' Tokyo, in Japantown, who snap up every copy of 'Japan Today' because they think Mrs. Narisato's reviews are going to become collector's items some day. A review by your grandmother, something like that."

I guess the puzzled expression on my face forced her to get a little deeper in her explanation.

"Look, I'm a fourth generation Japanese-American, Yonsei, if you wanted to get technical about it, who is definitely in touch with her roots and all that. So, when I first read Mrs. Narisato's restaurant reviews I found them . . . well, interesting."

I gave her a high five across my desk.

"But, how can I say it? Somewhat strange . . . maybe somewhat strange is a way of saying I almost died laughing. It was the way she used the English language. Please don't misunderstand me, there are people in my family who are still struggling to speak proper English, but they're not writing a restaurant review column in 'Japan Today.'

I was puzzled by the fact that the publishers, the editors of 'Japan Today' had obviously given Mrs. Narisato free play to write anything she wanted to write, in any way she wanted to write. After a couple issues I felt compelled to do a bit of investigating, I had to find out what the deal was."

"What did you do?"

"I used a few sheets of Department of Justice stationery to bamboozle my way into a meeting with Mr. Carl Kentaro, the publisher/editor of 'Japan Today.'

I was very upfront and open about my purpose for being there, to find out how Mrs. Narisato became the Jonathan Gold of 'Japan Today.'

I have to tell you, Verona, Mr. Kentaro actually looked relieved to be able to talk about his restaurant reviewer. He actually called for tea as he told me the story."

"Mrs. Narisato is 82 years old, very spry, and is a member of the Shakuhachi family, one of the great Samurai clans of Central Japan. Mrs. Narisato's grandfather was the founder/owner of 'Japan Today.' He was also the President –CEO of a number of multi-national corporations. A very wealthy and powerful man.

One day his granddaughter decided that she wanted to do restaurants reviews for 'Japan Today' and, of course, he gave her permission to do what she wanted to do. Mrs. Narisato's grandfather always allowed her to do whatever she wanted to do because she was the 'apple of his eye.'

Mr. Sato, the publisher/editor at that time, this was three years ago, before I came on board, and the staff were given instructions not to edit or bother Mrs. Narisato's contribution in any shape, form or fashion. It's been that way for the past two years. We have to suck the dust', as they say, because no one would dare think of causing Mrs. Narisato to lose face by suggesting that her English language skills are not quite up to the task of doing the restaurant reviews. We would not want to cause her unnecessary distress."

"What did he mean by that? To cause her 'to lose face,' to cause her unnecessary distress?"

Shirley went into a heavy thought mode for a moment or so before answering.

"I don't want to over dramatize this, but there is the possibility that 'losing face' might cause the old lady to commit Hari Kari . . . ."

"Hari Kari? Suicide? Are you kidding me?"

"I'm afraid not. There are some Japanese, 'specially in the older, more traditional frame of reference who still have a sense of honor that comes from another time. 'Loss of face might mean suicide'".

"Wowwww."

XXX    XXX

# CHAPTER 9

"So, HERE WE ARE, TWO years later, after reading Mrs. Narisato's review of Ichiban. Like I told Daniel, after reading the review, we have to take a trip to Ichiban. We did. And called you guys, raving about the food."

"Mrs. Narisato still writing her reviews?"

"Unfortunately no, we missed her in a couple issues and Shirley called Mr. Kentaro and found out that she had had a stroke and passed away."

"Sorry to hear that. Ahh hah, here we go, the sakizuke, the appetizer!"

XXX     XXX

### <u>Jonathan</u>

"Well, as Daniel can tell you, it's in my book, I had a patient expatriate himself and his wife to Denmark because they didn't feel that they could continue to live in a country where a man like Trump could possibly weasel himself into the presidency.

Win, lose or whatever, they just felt that he had shown us how much bigotry, racism, hatred and down right evil there was in our country. The way my friend Henry explained it to me – 'Look, Doc, if you live in a place where millions, millions of white folks, mostly, would be willing to give the leadership of the greatest country on Earth over to a pathological liar, a bona fide con man, a racist, basically a rotten human being, to put it bluntly, just because he promised to 'make America White again,' then I think that would be enough of a catalyst to anywhere that would <u>not</u> allow a Trump to plant his hate . . . ."

XXX     XXX

CoCo Chen-Lane; Hassun, 2$^{nd}$ course-Sushi
and some small side dishes . . . .

"I don't know who has been sleeping on this, but the head of our department recently issued a new guideline that makes it quite clear that there are no longer any norms for what might be considered 'abnormal behavior.' In other words, somebody has made a decision to equate craziness with normality . . . ."

"But that's, that's crazy, CoCo."

"I would definitely agree with you, but you would definitely have a whole bunch of other people who would disagree with you."

"Whooaa! Hold on here a second! CoCo, are you saying that people who might ordinarily be considered mentally ill would just fit right in with the rest of us?"

"Dan, read my lips – I'm not saying that. I'm saying that the memo that was passed down to us mental-health-care-peons made it clear that there were no longer any norms for what might be considered 'abnormal behavior.'"

"What's that going to do to the legal system? What happens when someone will no longer be able to cop a plea of innocence due to an attack of temporary insanity? Or insanity period."

"It does open a can of worms, doesn't it? O great! Here's the mukozuke, the sliced sashimi."

## XXX    XXX

Verona,

(Takiawase vegetables served with meat, fish, tofu, ingredients simmered separately.)

"Michelle Alexander's book, 'A New Jim Crow.' If you were thinking about what was terribly wrong with the legal system, especially how it relates to African-Americans and other people of color, read this lady's book."

"It's been on her bedside night stand ever since it was published."

"For someone involved with the so called justice system in this country, I feel obligated to read, to know as much as possible about how things work in the system. I have to be honest about it and tell you that there are some things we're doing to people of color and poor people in this great country that are absolutely shameful."

"So, it's really true that you need money to really get justice in America?"

"Add one or more factor, Jonathan, a pale skin will help the process a great deal."

XXX    XXX

They paused in their conversation to look around at the people who had filtered in. Experienced Ichiban restaurant people watchers, they didn't have to nudge each other or point at the interesting people in the tables all around them.

They were quite impressed by the six men and women who made a majestic entrance. Huge brown men and huge bronzed women, huge but not fat. The men wore gorgeously patterned lapas and the women were dressed in old fashioned muu muus, complete with lovely little hats. CoCo whispered, "Gauguin was right, they are beautiful people." Verona, Jonathan and Daniel nodded in silent agreement, each of them visualizing the lush tropical paintings of Paul Gauguin. Mexican families ordering pounds of fried fish. African-American teriyaki lovers. Anglo couples with cherubic blonde children. And scattered throughout the mix, Japanese using their chopsticks with surgical precision.

"Ahhh, the grilled fish, yakimono."

Their attention was diverted from people watching to the next item on the Kaiseki agenda. Just enough to really taste but not to be filled up with.

"I love the textures, the balanced flavors of this food," Daniel murmured as he expertly chopsticked a piece of grilled fish into his chops. Jonathan signaled to their waitress for another round of beer and tea.

XXX    XXX

Su-zakana, vegetables in vinegar to cleanse the palate.

"I can't make myself believe that there are still people in the government who do not believe in global warming."

83

"Verona, don't fool yourself, they <u>do</u> believe. The problem with them is that they've sold themselves so completely to the 'global warmers,' if you know what I mean, that they've been forced to take the most idiotic position any rational human being could take, I can't recall any other time in history quite like this."

XXX     XXX

Ko no mono/pickled vegetables

"I have to confess, I never even thought about a boxing match 'til Muhammad Ali danced onto the scene."

"CoCo, include your husband. I always thought it was the most brutal thing two men could do to each other, get into a squared ring and try to beat each other into unconsciousness . . . ."

"And that was true about Muhammad Ali too, ask Floyd Patterson, Joe Frazier, Sonny Liston and all of the others who had the nerve to climb into the ring with him."

"But he did it with so much grace and beauty."

"You can put it that way if you want to, CoCo. All I can say is this – getting your butt kicked by Muhammad Ali may have looked beautiful and graceful, but I'm sure it must've hurt a little bit, too."

"You can say that again. Are we ready for the misumono?"

"In a bit, I'd rather have another beer before we get into dessert . . . ."

XXX     XXX

They settled into a relaxed groove, fully enjoying the lingering flavors on their palates, the sights and sounds all around them. Jonathan and Daniel sipping their bottles of beer, savoring the subtle flavor of the well chilled Ichibans.

Verona and CoCo sipped their cups of scented tea as though it was a fine wine. Jonathan leaned across the table toward Daniel.

"Alright, Dan, now that you've had enough nutrition to fight off your weakness, what about this second story you were going to tell me?"

"What second story?"

84

"Well, as you know, Jonathan and I have been polishing up our autobiographies and sharing a few of the events we're writing about, that we've written about. He told me about this guy named Bob who seems to have time warped himself back into ancient Egypt . . . ."

"I think that's a very good way to phrase that, Dan."

CoCo Chen-Lane and Verona Obregon-Hoover listened to their husbands as though they were following a good tennis match. They loved to hear "their guys" exchange notes.

"So, what's this second story?" Verona nudged the pace.

Dan took a pregnant moment to prime his audience.

"This happened about five years ago. Sometimes I think of it as the year, the summer of that year when all of us went off somewhere . . . ."

"Five years ago? O yeah, that's when Jonathan went to Holland, to the Hague with Verona, to this conference on what to do with the global problem of abducted children, many of them being forced into the sex slave traffic . . . ."

"And it was the same year, the same summer, dear CoCo, that you tripped up to Sacramento, with a few hundred other Obama Healthcare professionals, to spend a week fighting off the attacks of a bunch of mis-informed, mis-guided, prejudiced, psuedo racist, semi-wannabe fascistic numbskulls, in what was supposed to be a bi-partisan conference."

CoCo clapped her hands, applauding her husband's beer fueled description of the conference she had attended.

"You didn't get it all exactly right, Dan, but you got the bullet points exactly right . . . ."

"So, whilst Jonathan and Verona were in Holland, at the Hague, CoCo was body slamming the neo-nuts – should I use another title?"

CoCo gave her husband a playful punch to the left shoulder.

"Husband, if you don't call them what they deserve to be called, I'm gonna float around you like a butterfly and sting you like a bee."

Jonathan and Verona egged the action onward by softly chanting: "Float around like a butterfly and sting like a bee . . . ."

Their waitress, mistaking their animated exchanges for attempts to grab her attention, rushed to their table with two more beers and tea. No one refused and simply smiled. Daniel was taking them into his second story.

## XXX    XXX

"To tell the absolute truth, if I hadn't been left on my own, completely deserted by my wife and friends,,,,"

CoCo, the wife, and Jonathan and Verona released their well-orchestrated groan of fake sympathy. Daniel used their reactions for theatrical effect.

"Completely deserted by my wife . . . ."

"Daniel, I called you three times a day and texted you in between times . . . ." He smiled her "alibi" away. This was his story and he was going to tell it his way.

"If I had had anyone around me to suggest that going to Beijing, for a three-day seminar on 'Spirit Points' in acupuncture, would be a bad idea, I might've gone anyway."

They all shared a laugh, knowing how stubborn Daniel Lane II could be.

"So, I went, our colleagues, Dr. Bao Xi, Dr. Shen Nong and Dr. Quan Yuangi were my gracious hosts . . . ."

"I remember all three of those men, they came during our third year in SoHMAA, very wise men, very wise . . . ."

"If you recall, they were very interested in establishing the reality of spirit acupuncture points . . . ."

Verona pursed her lips, frowned a bit.

"Whoooa, hold on a sec, guys, that's a new one for the attorney . . . spirit acupuncture points?"

"Jonathan, would you care to do the honors?"

"It's like this, Verona. Let's say someone has his left leg amputated, it's been proven that the amputee may still feel 'ghost nerves,' feeling from below the amputated area."

"Really?"

"Lots of documentation, but I'm a bit fuzzy about how acupuncture fits into this. Dr. Lane?"

"If you remember, Dr. Mehta and the rest of the staff were not exactly burning with passion for this particular aspect of acupuncture. Dr. Mai and Dr. Nordlung were firmly against it because they didn't feel enough data had been gathered to support an unequivocal acceptance of 'spirit points.'

Even as a young intern I disagreed with them. I felt that the 'spirit points' were as real as any of the other meridians; it was simply a matter of clearly defining them, doing the same thing that's been done with all the other meridians. Once they were clearly defined, they wouldn't seem so mysterious, so unusual.

The thing that pulled me off to the Beijing Seminar was the e-mail invitation from the doctors that stressed that they had been concentrating on the spiritual aspects, as related to the spirit points."

CoCo released a cynical laugh.

"That really sounds kind of funny to my Buddhist ears, that someone in atheistic mainland China should be talking about anything 'spiritual.'"

"CoCo, I gotta agree with you, sweetheart. But I also have to say that official policy, the government, doesn't have the power to shut down the feelings, the emotions of the average person.

Doctors Bao Xi, Shen Nong and Quan Yuangi are all Christians, that's what they told me privately. They may not go to Catechism or Sunday school, but they are Christians in faith. I suspect that their Christian faith was one of the catalysts for their research about spiritual points. No, Verona, they weren't trying to determine how many angels could fit on a pin head, or anything that medieval."

"Would you care for something more?"

The new waitress made a slight bow as she cleaned the table of beer bottles. Jonathan was on point.

"Yes, please give us another round."

"Thank you, sir."

"O.k., Dan, no angels on pin heads. Nothing weird."

"Nothing weird. Dr. Bao Xi started us off at noon on the first day with an hour long presentation. The basic point he made during his presentation was that acupuncture had too long been associated simply with the idea of alleviating pain. He made a brief to substantiate the possibility that there were other spheres to be explored, the purely spiritual, or as he put it – "The divinity that these spiritual points can connect us to."

I have to tell you, his presentation was not one of the quiet academic lectures. He was only five minutes into his spiel when some members of the audience began to act up. Dr. Shen Nong and Dr. Quan Yuangi did a great job of translating for a few minutes, until the hall became somewhat heated. It didn't take a lot of translation to determine that some of the people in the auditorium were not pleased with Dr. Bao Xi's premises, his presentation.

"Why only pain?" he asked at one point. "Acupuncture is magic of a wonderful sort, but why only pain?"

After a break for food, "snacks' they called the sumptuous spread we were served, Dr. Shen Nong took the podium. I think his presentation stepped up a bit from where Bao Xi had left us. Dr. Quan Yuangi alternately translated for me.

"I would like to have it clearly understood that the propositions that we are presenting should not be considered iron clad, propositions engraved in stone. In many cases I can cite, that I may cite, I shall simply say that we are working on this, that it is a work in progress. In other instances, I will be able to say – we have checked these out and there is a 199% chance of our findings being accurate."

"I liked the non-jargonistic approach that these men made to their subject. We are doctors and we could let fly with all of the jargon you could stand, but we won't go there. I thought that was quite cool."

"Ladies and gentlemen, I will repeat – when I say we have checked something out and that there is a 99% chance of it being accurate, trust me. Now then, I shall be carrying on past the point Dr. Bao Xi left us. Why <u>only</u> pain? That was the question uppermost in our minds when we started our research on the possibility of spiritual acupunctural points.

It seemed only natural to Dr. Bao Xi, Dr. Shen Nong and myself that there would have to be points to meridians that would lead us above and beyond the simple relief of lower back pain . . . ."

"There was something like a little giggle that swept thru the audience. Maybe something was lost in the translation, I didn't get it."

"Sometimes," he continued, "sometimes one must look in unfamiliar places to find answers. I took it upon myself to study several systems of spirituality before I came to the Yoruba, West African system, as a determining spiritual force. I cannot explain why, we're still working on this, but it stems from the fact that the Yoruba were there when there was a There There.

Or maybe, I can explain it this way; when the animal we call Man first stepped onto the front porch of his cave home, looked up into the sky, all around himself, and had the nerve or presence of mind to ask himself – who am I? And how do I fit into all of this? And what I do about it?

I cannot say what answers he gave himself because I wasn't there . . . and now, for the sake of the modern fixation on time, I will have to fast forward from that time to a time that I will call – a few eons ago. I have not found any incredible evidence that the Yoruba people of Nigeria were great carvers, wonderful painters, tremendous builders or anything like that, but apparently some of the questions that our cave man ancestor asked were given plausible answers by the Yoruba spiritual philosophers. Yes, Africa, the birthplace of the human species. It seems only reasonable when you think about it . . . if Africa is the Mother of the Earth's people. Then, is it not also reasonable and logical that the birth of what we call spirituality should also have occurred on that continent?"

"I couldn't tell if Dr. Shen Nong was just taunting his audience to contradict him, or if he was driving a point home. I could see frowns knit the brows of several people sitting near me."

"Why the Yoruba spiritual model became worldwide, either overtly or clandestinely, is a puzzle that we can wrestle with at a later time. What we do know is this: eons ago, most of the so called civilized nations of the Earth, the Romans, the Greeks, for example, embraced the Yoruba spiritual template, but changed the names to protect their identity theft – thus Obatalà became Zeus on Olympus and all that.

We can see evidence of identity theft or assimilation of the Yoruba system in most of the world's ancient religions. The latter day guys are a different story."

"I have to admit, he had me. Where was the this guy taking us?"

"Now, some of you are asking yourselves – where is this guy taking us?"

"I don't know if Dr. Shen Nong was a mind reader or not, but he stared right into my face when he posed the question, And there was a twinkle in his eyes."

CoCo, Verona and Jonathan smiled at Daniel's description of what happened.

"I will soon get to where I am taking you, soon, to prevent farther anxiety. Using the Yoruba spiritual system, a system that embraces a pantheon of what they call 'Orishas,' what some people would call 'Divinities' or 'Angels,' or 'helpers,' I determined that these Orishas were meridians to specific types of spirituality.

I cannot say that I discovered anything, I shall simply say that diligent study and perseverance made me <u>aware</u> that there were spiritual forces that could be tapped for relief of problems, for advice about medical problems, for advice about what to eat and drink, about how to live a sweeter life.

If the Yoruba way was approached with sacrifices, with singing, drumming, dancing and the right sacrifices, then why not find out if appeals could be made for a sweeter life by other means? As a Chinese man, a doctor, I asked myself – if there are an unlimited number of ways to find peace, love, even happiness . . . then why shouldn't acupuncture be used to seek these states of being?"

Daniel paused to take a sip of his beer. Verona leaned forward with her elbows on the table. This was becoming interesting.

"As I said earlier, I have never believed that our acupuncture was developed solely for the relief of lower back pain . . . ."

Once again there was that little wave of insider-giggling.

"So, I began to work with my colleagues, Dr. Bao Xi and Dr. Quan Yuangi, to determine how we could use our acupuncture expertise to achieve higher spiritual planes. Dr. Quan Yuangi will take us onward."

"They moved like a well-rehearsed dance team. Dr. Quan was a small, quick moving old man. He looked to be about sixty. I found out after the seminar that he was ninety two."

"Dr. Nong has left the hard part for me. O.k., I'm up to the challenge . . . ."

"I loved the humor these men exchanged, the way they played with their audience."

"First off, let me say that we discovered, early on, that the Orishas are not 'gods,' as some people, including many of our African brothers and sisters, believe. Instead, we discovered, paying close attention to the original concept of what an 'Orisha' is supposed to be, that an Orisha represents a principle and that principle can only be arrived at by using the correct approach, the correct road, the best meridian.

Please allow me to use one example; let us say that someone has a problem that needs to be solved. This person will go to a qualified priest, the priest will do a 'reading' for this person. The priest may use methods of divination that are not fully understood in the West. Or East either.

One of the methods of divination utilizes cowrie shells. Ifa divination is complex and requires the abilities of a qualified person. The analogy that I might use is what happens when someone goes to a qualified acupuncturist.

In the case of the person going to the Yoruba priest, a man is called a BaBalawo, a woman is called an Iyalosha, an appeal may be made to a chosen Orisha. Let us say that the appeal (for a solution of the problem) is made to the Orisha Eshu, the 'deity' of the crossroads.

As you can hear, I'm qualifying words like 'gods,' 'deities,' 'divinities,' etc. etc., because different cultures have different understandings of the same word. In any case, if the proper formula for the solution of the problem has been determined, which means, in this case, a sacrifice to Eshu, the Lord of the crossroads, and giving up eating pork . . . ."

"I heard something like a collective groan swell up from the audience. Dr. Bao Xi whispered, in between the lines of his translation, 'you know how much we Chinese love our pork.'"

"The sacrifices to Eshu will enable the person making the appeal to have a resolution to his/her problem . . . ."

The good doctor paused for a full thirty seconds, surveying his audience like a master actor.

"One of the premises in our work has been to find a higher spiritual plane, a way, by way of acupuncture to locate and activate those spiritual forces that exist in all of us, forces that may be dormant, stagnant, but are there nevertheless.

We are not seeking to put our African brothers and sisters out of work, we are simply making efforts to 'spiritualize' our Chinese acupuncture, to help our patients achieve greater unity with certain spiritual principles. I will say – love, first off. Peace. Great inner harmony. A sense of human-ness that would prohibit us from killing each other. The cleansing of disease from our bodies and the atmosphere. A sense of what a beautiful life is supposed to be. I could go on and on and on.

Spiritually, we are making an effort to do with the acupuncture needles what the Yoruba priest is doing with his/her readings, her prayers, her advice about which sacrifice should be made to achieve the best results.

91

Who knows? Maybe some day we will be able to blend our techniques and elevate the human species to a higher spiritual level."

"He went on for a bit more, but that was the core of his talk, of what they talked about . . . ."

"That's quite a story . . . ."

"Sorry, Jonathan, that's just the first part of the story, there's more."

"There's more?"

"Yep, there's more."

"Well, hold on for a minute, I gotta go mail a letter."

They shared smiles, watching Jonathan dodge toddlers roaming the restaurant aisles, politely wedge his way thru to the men's room. Verona pursed her lips, her usual prelude to a question.

"Dan, you've told me about the seminar, but what's this about more to that story?"

"I'll tell you in a minute, I gotta go mail a letter, too."

XXX    XXX

# CHAPTER 10

"AFTER THE SEMINAR WAS OVER, the good doctors took me to the Golden Duck. I thought the sumptuous spread, no other word fits the description of what was buffeted in front of me, that we had had earlier, was wonderful. The food at the Gold Duck was incredible. All I can remember, as one delicious dish after another was whirled around in front of me, is a feeling of complete indulgence.

The seminar was discussed for a minute or two before the waiters began to serve and thereafter it was flying chopsticks. Dr. Bao Xi, Dr. Shen Nong and Dr. Quan Yuangi were thin as rails and ate like heavy duty laborers. The dinner went on for about two hours and strangely, at the conclusion, I didn't feel stuffed. I'm sure it had a lot to do with the heavy vegan base of what we ate.

'As you can see, Dr. Lane, we Chinese love to eat. Or as one of my colleagues put it – 'we Chinese eat to love.' Hahhahahah.'

We were scheduled to hear more about the work that the three doctors were doing the next afternoon. They offered to give me a little guided tour of Beijing in the mornings before the lecture. I vetoed the guided tour.

'Gentlemen, I appreciate your offer, but I would prefer being directed to the nearest flea market, so that I can find that bargain item I'm not looking for.'

We went 'round about this for about a half hour, 'til I came to the conclusion that I was fighting a losing battle. They were not going to allow me to wander around anywhere by myself. I think they were afraid that something would happen to me, that there might be an 'incident'.

We compromised. They produced a man named 'Mr. Hai Xing.' A guy who looked like he had been lifting weights for a while, and had stumbled into a few fists, nose first, in his young life.

'Mr. Hai Xing will accompany you, he will help you get what you want. He is very good at bargaining.'

It didn't take a lot of effort to see that they had supplied me with a bodyguard who could scare would be criminals away from me. And, incidentally, help me buy what I wanted. He also spoke a few words of English. O well, it was all good. Off we tripped.

I would never be able to say where we went, which section of the city Mr. Hai Xing ('not too bad') drove us to, but when we got there I was in a Chinese thrift shopper's paradise.

Block after block was filled with all kinds of stuff; pottery on this block, clothes, cheap and expensive, in the next block, old stuff, new stuff. It didn't take me long to fill up Mr. Hai Xing's muscular arms with stuff that I had acquired with his 'bargaining ability.'

It reached the point where Mr. Hai Xing was forced to admit he couldn't carry all of my stuff, and he wouldn't allow me to lift a finger to help him.

'Doctor, you stay here I go to car. O.k.?'

'O.k.'

He deposited all of my stuff in front of a small shop. People looked at me as he lumbered away, but no one spoke. I guess it was obvious that I was under the protection of Big Brother, in the most literal sense of the word. It only took a minute of window shopping for me to decide that I wanted to go inside this shop. What should I do about the stuff piled up beside me on the sidewalk? The shop owner, an old man who looked like a piece of dried parchment, had been studying me as I window shopped. He beckoned for me to come in and sent a young man, his son maybe, outside to guard my stuff. It was all done with gestures and body language. What did I need with a Mr. Hai Xing?

Mr. Wu Nánrén made a slight bow in my direction and gracefully led me from section to section of his shop. It was much larger inside than it seemed to be on the outside."

Daniel took notice of the way Verona's lips were pursed, her prelude to asking a question. And Jonathan was tapping his right forefinger on the edge of the table.

"To make a long story short, Mr. Nánrén led me into a back room that was stacked half way to the ceiling with boxes, beautifully lacquered, gorgeously decorated boxes."

'Chinese box, you want?' He spoke to me in an urgent tone. I didn't have to be asked twice. I paid a ridiculously small amount of money for nine of the boxes.

"I send?' he asked, gesturing with his chin in the direction of Mr. Hai Xing had gone. I got it. He was suggesting that I wouldn't have to tell Mr. Hai Xing what I had done. I liked the idea of doing something without Big Brother's 'help.'

'Yes, send.' I gave him my card and got back out onto the sidewalk just as my guide-translator-bodyguard was pulling up.

'Don't worry, sir, we send o.k.' The old man spoke inn a coarse whisper. 'I'm sure you will.'

It took me a quick minute of reflection, once my stuff was loaded, to reach the conclusion that I had been scammed.

What if Mr. Nánrén and son had simply decided to take my money and not send the boxes? O, well, it was only fifty bucks. That was a consolation. It could've been a hundred."

XXX   XXX

"As you all can recall, I was back home about three weeks before my shipment of boxes arrived . . . ."

"I know, we all got one. My question concerns the last day of the 'spiritual acupuncture' lectures. What did they say? What did they reveal?"

"Excellent questions, Doctor Hoover, excellent questions. I can answer you by saying that Doctor Bao Xi, Doctor Shen Nong and Doctor Quan Yuangi found a sort of fifty-fifty acceptance of the theories that they were promoting. I say fifty/fifty because of the vibes I felt around me. Let me give you an example or two."

"I address my question to the esteemed Doctor Shen Nong. 'You say that you are in support of Doctor Quan Yuangi, and Doctor Bao Xi, with their suggestions that our five-thousand-year-old history of acupuncture should be linked to the primitive history of savage Africa . . . ?'"

'Please stop there, Chinese racist-brotherman; if you are not willing to recognize the place that Africa has played in the development of human history, then you must be considered a disciple of the Anglo-American politician called Trump.'

"I have to admit, I was a bit dazzled and puzzled by the exchanges that happened. It was all quite 'civilized,' but there was an edge to things."

"So, you are saying that our great Chinese cultural tradition of acupuncture lacks emotion, lacks spiritual content?"

"No, not entirely, my young friend.' It didn't take an intimate knowledge of Chinese to get the feel of how Doctor Bao Xi slowly bored into this question."

"No, my young friend, I'm not saying that our great Chinese cultural tradition of acupuncture lacks emotion or spiritual content. We are simply trying to make a case for having a greater development of what we may already have. And, if the catalyst for this development stems from our African research . . . well, I would suggest you accept reality and forget about racial fantasies."

"Racial fantasies." I don't think I've ever heard that connected series of bat wing-wing nut words used so eloquently. Hey, forget your "Celestial Kingdom" view of the world pal. It didn't start with us, it took place on the 'Dark Continent,' which wasn't so 'Dark' when you begin to study what the real deal is, has been."

I felt a bit "wrung out" when the afternoon was over. "Wrung Out," a term one of my graduate students used to use when we had shared a particular piece of grueling scholastic investigation.

I was really pleased that I had been able to hear the lectures of Doctors – Bao Xi, Shen Nong and Quang Yuangi – and sample the vibes of present day China for a few days and get back home.

XXX    XXX

"I had a very nervous three weeks waiting for my lacquered boxes to arrive . . . ."

"He was meeting the postman at the front gate every morning."

"I guess I did seem a little anxious, but I was looking forward to giving you guys your presents . . . ."

"Really 'ppreciate it, Dan, they're really beautiful. I keep my jewelry in mine . . . ."

"And I use mine to store the household bills. So, that's the story, huh?"

"Not quite, Verona, not quite. The story came out of the box that I saved for myself. Beautiful box . . . ."

"They <u>are</u> beautiful."

"Blonde wood, lightly tinted red and yellow. I think I must've spent some part of every day, just staring at this beautiful box on my desk for a week after it arrived."

Daniel's narrative was interrupted by a loud discussion in the next booth. Two men were having an argument about who should pay the bill for their food and drinks.

"No! No! No! Frank, you paid the check the last time! This one is on me! Take your credit card back! Take it back!"

"I will not take it back! I'm going to pay for this one!"

Their waitress, a young Japanese woman with an innocent looking baby face, made a suggestion.

"Gentlemen, may I make a suggestion?"

The persistent "bill collectors" stared at the young woman for a hard moment. They were two inebriated Anglo-upper middle guys who wanted to do a credit card duel. En garde!

"Yeah, go ahead young lady, make a suggestion."

"I will flip a coin to determine who will pay the check this time. And the other person will pay the check the next time."

The antagonists, a bit bleary eyed from Ichiban sushi and well chilled Sapporos, nodded in agreement. The waitress assigned "heads/tails" and flipped a quarter. All of us craned our necks to see who had won the right to pay. The one called Frank won the toss.

Daniel returned to his own business with renewed interest.

"It got to the point where I actually felt that this box was talking to me . . . ."

"Daniel, my darling, remember – you're talking to Jonathan, Verona, and your lawfully bewedded wife, CoCo. We are not easily convinced box speakers, of my boxes that speak."

"CoCo, I'm serious. Well, who am I talking to? You were the first one I came to with this letter I pulled out of a secret compartment in the box."

"It was a small scroll covered with Chinese calligraphy."

"What did it say, CoCo?"

CoCo Shen-Hoover hesitated to answer, obviously reluctant to respond to Verona's question.

"Look, let me say this. I'm Chinese to the core, that's the way I feel, who I am. But I have to be honest and say that I had a strong sense of anti-Chinese sentiment in me for a long time, that had to do with what the Chinese did to my grandparents in 1949. This is when Mao unleashed the Red Guards on the country. The Red Guards tortured and murdered my grandparents, on my father's side, because they were musicians/music teachers who gave instructions about 'decadent Western music.' And murdered my grandparents, on my mother's side because they had spent vacations in 'decadent France.' Hope anyone can understand that?

Dan helped me to get past what would've been self-hatred when he reminded me that it was the Chinese government, under Mao, who had caused all of my grandparents to be slaughtered like pigs.

So, what am I saying? I took a long, careful look at the scroll and suggested that it should be translated by a "worthy person". I could make out the bare bones of what was on the scroll, but I didn't feel that I could give a realistic translation/interpretation."

We went 'round 'n 'round for a few days about this. Anybody know anybody who could translate some ancient Chinese script into modern English? You wanna believe this? From out of Nowhere, this young African-American woman named Krystal put in an appearance.

Why lie about it? We were floored! An African-American woman who spoke, could read, could write, could translate this scroll we had. It would save us the effort of going to the professionals. But first we had to test her capabilities. She knocked us out of the box by offering us her Ph.D. treatise, written in Mandarin. She could write in Chinese.

She had done extensive reading of Chinese Literature, both Ancient and Modern. And she knew something about acupuncture. What could I say?! We were on.

The week after I had given her this long thing to translate, she e-mailed – "Dr. Lane, this is a pleasure to translate. We can meet at your convenience – Krystal Long."

"We invited her over and had an absolutely delightful afternoon of tea sipping and conversation. Nosy CoCo just had to find out how Krystal became interested in Chinese."

"I felt <u>compelled</u> to find out how she had become so proficient in Chinese. I mean, let's face it, there are a whole bunch of Chinese people, including myself, who have a hard time reading and writing Mandarin. And here is this young African-American woman, how old . . .?"

"Twenty-four years old, from Athens, Georgia, of all places, and completely at ease with the language. The only explanation she could give us was that she became interested in Chinese culture back in grammar school. Her parents sponsored her to four – five trips to China in her teens and the die was cast.

This is what she translated from the scroll. I don't have the hard copy of what she translated, so I'll para-phrase. CoCo, check me out so that I don't miss anything."

"No problem . . . ."

"The actual story starts off in the early years of the Qing Dynasty, 1644-1911."

"Wowww! That far back?"

"Jonathan, my jaw dropped too. That's right – 1644 something. It seems that acupuncture and moxibustion were in fashion, approved of, officially. These elements were included in a special section of something called 'the Golden Mirror of Medicine,' or as Krystal called it, 'Yizong Injian,' a 90 volume work.

But then, in 1822, the Emperor Dao Guang issued an imperial edict stating that acupuncture and moxibustion were not suitable forms of treatment for a ruler and should be banned forever from the Imperial Medical Academy. The most reasonable reason for this, according to Krystal, is that the Emperor was fearful of being assassinated. Most of the doctors were Han and they weren't trusted."

"As a modern parallel, think of Stalin and the Jewish physicians who were given such a rough time during that era."

"I get it. Go on, this is fascinating."

"Fast forwarding a bit. Krystal made it clear, from her translation/ interpretation, that this scroll was probably written by someone who opposed the Emperor's Edict. And then she really blew our own minds by asking – "Have you gone thru all of the compartments in the box?"

"All of the compartments in the box?" We stared at her like complete idiots . . . ..

CoCo laughed out loud, rare thing for her to do.

"That's a good description, Dan, a very good description."

"Krystal made a very careful study of the box, somewhat like someone meditating. She pressed on the six tiers in the box. We thought that were only three tiers, three slim drawers. She studied the box for about ten minutes longer before she used both thumbs to press on the east and west corners of the box, very gently.

A very thin drawer slowly slid open and inside were nine golden acupuncture needles."

Verona and Jonathan repeated what they had just heard, in tandem-chorus.

"Nine golden acupuncture needles?"

"Nine gold needles. I counted them about five times. Krystal went on to say that these needles had probably been hidden as an act of rebellion against the Emperor Dao Guang's edict. As we all know, from the 18th century onward, when acupuncture became well known to the west, the whole system of Chinese medicine was designated a national cultural heritage and it's been on a roll since then."

"So, what happened to the needles?"

"Exactly the same question I would've asked you, Doctor Hoover."

"Well . . .?"

"I gave it a lot of thought."

"<u>We</u> gave it a lot of thought."

"I, we decided that the only right thing to do was to return the needles to China, to the shop owner, Mr. Wu Nánrén.

Krystal helped us compose a very nice letter to Dr. Bao Xi, Dr. Shen Nong and Dr. Quan Yuangi, requesting their aid for the return of the box.

It took less than a day for them to e-mail a reply. They had questioned my bodyguard/guide, Mr. Hai Xing, and he had <u>assured</u> them that I had not purchased anything from any shop owner named Wu Nánrén. CoCo, you want to fill in the rest?"

"The reply was really puzzling for a few days, 'til it came to me like a flash. The old regime was still the old regime. Of course the guide/bodyguard would deny that he had let Daniel out of sight long enough to do anything on his own. What's it called, Verona, legally?"

"Dereliction of duty is one definition, or maybe criminal negligence."

"I'd make it a combination of both, enough to get you a long term stay in a Chinese penitentiary."

"And basically that's where it ended, almost. The problem I had was, I guess, a moral problem. I didn't really feel that I had a right to these precious needles just because an old man had made mistake. CoCo suggested that I go to see Dr. Mehta about the problem."

"I knew, if anyone could solve his moral dilemma it would be her."

"So I went. She listened closely, asked a bunch of very pertinent questions, like: "Was it your intention to defraud anybody when you went into this man's shop?" The answer was, of course, no.

We ying yanged it back and forth for about an hour before she gave her opinion.

"Daniel, if I were you, here's what I would do. Unless I could locate the <u>original</u> owner of these needles, I would keep them. You purchased a lacquered box, completely unaware that there were things concealed in the box. That box and all that was in it belong to you. Feel blessed."

"And that's where things are today."

"Wowww, now that's a story."

"Incidentally, Jonathan, if you want to use these needles sometimes, let me know."

"I'll take you up on that, Dan, I definitely will."

XXX    XXX

# CHAPTER 11

THEY STOOD IN THE PARKING lot of the Ichiban restaurant, bubbling with good vibes, reluctant, as usual, to call it a day.

"Jonathan, CoCo, are we playing doubles at the club on Wednesday evening>"

"We'll be playing. Hopefully you guys will be up to the challenge."

They loved to do that teasing-friendship thing with each other. Usually it involved their couples/double tennis matches. Not taken too seriously because they sometimes traded partners. A serious expression on Jonathan's face suddenly changed the mood of the moment.

"Dan, you know something? I've been thinking real hard on those 'acupuncture stories.' Thinking real hard. I think we ought to collaborate, combine our stories, have them published together because we seem to be more about the people we've treated than we are about ourselves."

CoCo and Verona high fived each other, they were immediately enthusiastic about the idea.

"Hey guys, that would be great!"

## XXX    XXX

By the end of their Wednesday evening doubles match, they had worked out the basic format for a book that their wives had come up with.

"'Ancestral Meridians,' that's the only reasonable name a reasonable person could call this collaboration . . . ."

Daniel Lane and Jonathan Hoover, familiar with their wives reasonable suggestions, playfully offered alternative titles.

"Ancestral Meridians? How about, 'Needles, Anyone?"

"Or 'The Acupunctural Moment?'"

"Daniel, I got a better one – 'The Emperor's Needles.'"

It took CoCo and Verona a few moments to realize that their joking-doctor-husbands were putting them on. It didn't take long for the men to admit that they couldn't come up with a better name than "Ancestral Meridians."

After a couple more months of re-writing, to form smoother transitions from story to story – "Let's alternate, Dan, starting with your man in Egypt."

"Good idea . . . ."

XXX    XXX

"So, how is he taking it?"

"You know how those guys are, they never surrender and they never admit that something is bugging them."

"What's the count now?"

"Fourteen rejections in eighteen months."

"Right, fourteen. I think they did a smart thing by dividing the submissions between them, seven each. I hate to think of how it would've made Daniel feel to receive fourteen rejections, one right after another."

"Same for Jonathan. What's with these publishing houses anyway? Here's a beautifully written book, filled with exciting, unusual material and they offer the most inane reason for rejecting the book that I've heard of.

Remember the one from Sutton House?"

"How could I forget it. I have it right in front of me – "Dr. Hoover, Dr. Lane, although we find your material esoteric, and somewhat compelling, we cannot think of a demographic that would be substantial enough to justify a Sutton House release.

We appreciate your interest in Sutton House and we wish you luck with your 'Ancestral Meridians.' Best, Gregory Raton."

"That one makes me smile, but this one, the letter from the agent pulls me in two directions, makes me want to smile and cry at the same time."

"Read it to me, CoCo."

"'Doctor Lane, Doctor Hoover,

I feel I would be able to get your book out there, onto the desks of the most influential editors in town, if you could sex up the content a bit. For example; are your female patients sometimes nude when you

103

are performing your needle tricks on them? There are other questions I could ask you in that vein, but I think you get the idea. Please feel free to reconnect with me if you are willing to take a few more suggestions, Sincerely, Mortimer Dutton, agent.'"

"O yes, that's one of my favorites too. I think he was thinking about a porno acupuncture novel, or maybe a porno funny book with needles stuck in it."

"Yeah, that seems to fit his mindset."

Verona Obregon-Hoover and CoCo Chen-Lane, concerned wives of two wannabe published authors, fell into an awkward, frustrated pause.

"CoCo . . . ."

"Yeah, Verona, I'm here."

"Girlfriend, listen closely. I've been doing a bit of research and let me tell you what I've discovered."

CoCo smiled at the sudden urgency in her friend's voice. If Verona Obregon-Hoover said she had discovered something, it was worth listening to.

"I have to say that the catalyst for this discovery came about after reading one of those weird, mindless, nutty rejection notices – 'We regret to inform you that Charter House does not accept material about ancient knitting techniques, blah, blah, blah.'

I started asking myself – what the hell is a publishing house? What're the elements that make up a publishing house? Who, what is a publisher? You know what I found out?"

"No, quick, tell me."

"I found out that the only thing you need to do to get into game is a business license from City Hall."

"Verona, you're kiddin'! That's all you need?"

"That's all we need, CoCo, that's all we need. There are probably a few other loose ends to be tied up, but that business license is the key."

"So, Kosmic Muffin Publishing House will be the place where 'Ancestral Meridians' is first published?"

"Exactly. What did you call it? Kosmic Muffin Publishing? I love it. Where did you get that from?"

"Just something that popped in my head. Seems to fit the nature of the thing, you know, a Kosmic happenin'."

"Love the concept. Well, let's get busy."

"What do we say to Dan and Jonathan?"

"Let's not say anything to them until we get the whole set up in place."

"Good idea. Let's meet and work out a few details about who is going to be responsible for doing what."

"Great! How 'bout the Café Oro at 10 a.m. on Saturday?"

"Café Oro at 10 Saturday. Verona, I'm glad you made your discovery. These guys have worked like dogs to put 'Ancestral Meridians' together, I think they deserve all the help we can give them."

"I'm already working on an acceptance letter to them . . . ."

"Love it, bye now – Café Oro at 10!"

XXX     XXX

"Jonathan, our wives are up to something . . . ."

"I know."

"What do you mean, you know?"

"Dan, I can't say that I can read Verona's mind or anything like that, but I do know, when I begin to see that focused gleam in her eyes – something's brewing."

"What do you think it is?"

"Hard to say about those two, they have so much imagination."

The two men, unhurried, reflective, stared at the summer sun slowly settling down thousands of miles away from them, shading the blue waters of the Pacific with tints of Gaugin yellow, Van Gogh reds, Arctic whites, rippling effect greens.

Old friends, they could speak inn a shorthand dialect that none but their wives could understand.

"CoCo, did Daniel tell you that he was meeting with Jonathan about a new project?"

"He might've mentioned it in passing, but you know how they are, they'll use any excuse to get together to watch the sun go down up there on the hill."

"You got that right!"

XXX     XXX

"It's a little like sipping a fine wine . . . ."

"You're absolutely right. Sometimes, when I've taken the time to read wine reviews – they have a guy in the Trader Joe's Express, Robert something or other – who gives you the weirdest ideas about how a particular wine is supposed to taste. 'There is the hint of strawberries,' he says . . . ."

"Yeah, yeah, I know who you're talking about. Verona trips on him."

"Strawberries, with hints of juicy coosie nuts and Bongo Bongo Marshmallow-jiggig-fruit. By the time he finishes giving out all of this extremely esoteric information about this bottle of wine, of excellent wine that we've had at dinner – with no hints of strawberries, coosie nuts, whatever the hell they are, or marshmallow jiggig fruit, there are times when I want to scream – Stop! You crazy ass fool! The wine is the wine! There are no hints of anything in it, other than what your taste tells you. And certainly not strawberries, coosie nuts, or marshmallow jiggig fruit!"

Daniel shook his head and smiled indulgently at his friend's rant.

"Uhhh, Jonathan, I think I pushed your rant button when I was about to suggest that watching the sunset from here, especially from this point on the hill, was a little like sipping a fine wine. Let's call it a fine visual wine. You buy that?"

Jonathan hung his head for a few beats. Daniel was right again, no need to compare the sublime with the pedestrian. If that was what the comparison offered by a wine taster with what they were experiencing could be considered, then the wine taster, Robert something or other, would definitely be lower casted.

"Yeahhh, I hear you, Daniel. I hear you. It would be, I don't know how you could put it; it would be dammed near impossible to compare a fine wine, maybe any wine, to what this is like."

"Hey, feel blessed that we're able to experience this . . . ."

"And to understand it!"

They high fived each other and settled back on their Signal Hill stone benches to watch the end of the day's sunset color/spiritual drama, play itself down.

### XXX    XXX

It took Verona Obregon-Hoover and CoCo Chen-Lane about three hard working months to put the Kosmic Muffin Press into being.

Meanwhile, Jonathan and Daniel had accumulated two more rejection slips –

"Dear Doctor Hoover - Doctor Lane, we seldom receive manuscripts like yours, that is to say, so well detailed, so richly researched. However, unfortunately, we must inform you that our editorial board has decided that it would not be in our best marketing interests to publish 'Ancestral Meridians' at this time. Thank you for giving us the opportunity to consider your interesting work – Best, Sidney Woolsworth, Publisher."

XXX    XXX

"Doctor Hoover-Lane,

Thank you for thinking of us, but we must inform you that we are not interested in any material that maybe so far out of the mainstream as to be considered unmarketable. Sincerely yours,

Mystri Havingstone-Wellworth."

XXX    XXX

"CoCo, Verona, let's hit this again. You're telling us that you two want to publish 'Ancestral Meridians'?"

"Yes, we are the Kosmic Muffin Publishing Company and, as you can see, we have already sent you two an acceptance letter for 'Ancestral Meridians.' We are quite familiar with the work and we believe, with the unique marketing techniques that we have put in place, that the book will be a best seller within a year or less."

Jonathan and Daniel stirred their Kenyan blend coffees in a subconscious counter clockwise motion. So, this is why they wanted to meet with us at the Café Oro. CoCo, the mental healthcare expert, picked up on their vibes and decided to go for the jugular.

"Look, guys, you've spent a lot of time and effort trying to get Hutton and Button, Double Day, Brown and Smith, and a bunch of other so called mainstream publishers to accept your manuscript, right?"

Jonathan and Daniel traded coded glances. Yes, she's right. Daniel answered for both of them.

"Uhhh, yes, CoCo, the answer is yes . . . ."

"So,' she sliced into what he was about to say; "So, that just goes to show how narrow minded and short sighted those people are. The Kosmic Muffin Publishing House is 'way ahead of al of those fuddy duddies and we're prepared to prove it."

Jonathan felt compelled to argue the point.

"CoCo, Verona, you may have your hearts in the right place, but this is not about hearts, sentimentality and all that, we're talking about cold blooded reality."

"What the hell do you think we're talking about Dr. Hoover?"

Once again, Jonathan and Daniel traded coded glances. They were being emotionally cornered. The tinkle clink of coffee cups, the register ringing, the business of the Café flowed around their encounter/discussion for a few beats as Jonathan and Daniel made a serious commitment/ decision.

The eye code appointed Daniel to be the spokesman for the duo.

"Awright, let's say we give our manuscript over to this Kosmic Muffin Press that you guys are talking about, what if it fails?"

CoCo Chen-Lane cut her husband's retreat off at the pass.

"Daniel, Jonathan, it can't fail. Here are the reasons why. Number one, you two have written a world class work. Do you doubt that?"

Jonathan and Daniel stirred their coffees around self-consciously.

"If you think you've done anything less than that," CoCo drove on, "then let's ring the curtain down right here." She allowed them a ten-second pause before she moved on.

"Now then, Kosmic Muffin has a world class work that we are going to market. Bottom line, you're giving us a chance to prove our worth and we're going to prove worthy of that trust."

It took a hard driving six months before superior material and dynamite marketing techniques began to put Jonathan Hoover, Daniel Lane and the Kosmic Muffin out there.

Jonathan and Daniel discussed the situation often . . . .

"Daniel, can you believe? These women are kicking asses and taking names."

"That's what they said they were going to do."

"And they're doing it. What time is our radio interview?"

"Four p.m., the KLBP station, 99.1"

"O yeah, this is third time for us with them. And don't forget, tomorrow we do the TV book show with that sour faced ol' man who asks such interesting questions. . . ."

"Witherspoon and books."

"That's the one. He's a sour puss but he does his homework and he does ask very interesting questions.

XXX   XXX

"CoCo, you believe this? Those guys have taken up to the p.r. circuit like seasoned vets."

"Verona, I think they're having fun. They're such pranksters. Remember the TV book show, hosted by whatshisname?"

"Mr. Wilhelm Witherspoon and books. How could I <u>not</u> remember it? They did so many puns, made so many sarcastic remarks, put the guy on so much I thought he would kick them out of the studio. But he <u>loved</u> it. He totally <u>loved</u> it. I think it was probably the first time anyone had ever come on his show and had fun, made fun of what he was doing."

"Remember Mr. Wilhelm Witherspoon asking them – "Now, Dr. Lane, Dr. Hoover, please tell us what acupuncture does, that traditional medicine doesn't do?""

"They answered the question as though they had rehearsed it a hundred times. Daniel took the first part and Jonathan came in with, "Well, Mr. Wilhelm Witherspoon," Daniel sliced the man's name up into fine distinct parts, "I think that we have to reverse your question, in order to answer it . . . .""

And Jonathan sarcastically eased in, obliquely; "We're the traditionalists here, what are those other people about?"

"Mr. Wilhelm Witherspoon stared at the two of them for a few beats, blinked like he had something in his left eye, and gave this big, thin lipped smile. But he didn't repeat the question backward or any other kind of way, he just moved on to the next question"

"What do you think it's about, Mr. Witherspoon? Obviously you haven't read it or you wouldn't be asking us what it's about. What do <u>you</u> think it's about?"

Verona and CoCo had "policy" meetings to try to determine what they could say to these two characters who seemed to be doing a literary Groucho Marx act selling their book.

"CoCo, what do you say to them?"

"What can you say? The book is becoming a critical/popular success, based largely on these 'unorthodox' interview that they're giving."

"Have you heard the latest?"

"No, what? Where?"

"They were doing the usual TV literary blah blah blah hosted by this woman who didn't know spit about acupuncture, who asked – 'does acupuncture hurt?'"

"Daniel asked; 'Do you want it to hurt?' followed by Jonathan saying, 'I'm feeling you, I'm feeling you.'"

"These guys are having 'way too much fun."

"Let 'em have all the fun they want, the Kosmic Muffin Publishing House money is rolling in."

It took them a full year, after the quirky television interviews, the zany radio interviews – "where are the cameras? We thought we were coming to be inter-viewed, not audio-taped" – to be fully out of the box. They were not two stuffy, jargon talking, middle aged alternative medical doctors trying to convince anybody of anything, they were just themselves, Daniel Lane and Jonathan Hoover. And the public loved that.

"Dan, Jonathan, we've had to hire someone to deal with your Facebook-fan mail . . . ."

The Kosmic Muffin Publishing House was rolling. Just before it hit the first curve, they made the decisions.

"Jonathan, Daniel, we want your advice about three decisions we want to make. Number one; should we 'go big' or stay in the 'boutique mode'? Two, we'd like to start the New Year off with another Hoover-Lane work. Any ideas about that? Number three, we want Krystal Long aboard to translate 'Ancestral Meridians' into Chinese. We think that we could tap into a huge market in China, Taiwan, Macao, wherever there is a large Chinese speaking population."

Daniel and Jonathan pretended that they were falling off of their chairs. Daniel was the first to recover.

"Let's start with the last question first. Me and Jonathan were talking about this up on the Hill yesterday morning, about getting into the Chinese speaking market. You can put Krystal to work today if you want to . . . ."

"Uhhh, we put her to work last week. We thought you two would like the idea of a little Chinese exposure. Also, we've engaged our book cover artist to do colored sketches to accompany the text."

"Zola Lin?! How did you manage to get hold of her, she's always off somewhere."

"Question two. Jonathan?"

"Concerning the new work for the New Year, you two have not been the only ones moving rapidly. We're into a new work we're calling 'Internal Discussions.' (Third work, 'Needles, Cupping Herbs', etc., etc., etc."

"I like that, we like that!"

"Finally, concerning the size of things. Verona, CoCo, you two have really convinced us that you could take us to the moon if you really wanted to."

CoCo and Verona made shy smiles, really delighted by the praise that Daniel was laying on them.

"But, we don't want to go to the moon. We'd like to remain Earthbound, which means 'boutique small.' Let's say Kosmic Muffin would be responsible for putting out four – six books a year, including our latest. How 'bout that?"

They sealed the deal with a four-cup toast – "to the Kosmic Muffin Publishing House!"

XXX    XXX

# CHAPTER 12

### From my Great Grandfather's Eyes

"SAM, COME SIT OUT ON the porch with me, there are a few things I want to talk about, to share with you before I kick the bucket."

"Awwww c'mon, grandpa, you're not gonna die . . . ."

"Well, I don't plan to die, but how many normal people <u>plan</u> to die" It's something that happens to all of us, sooner or later."

I joined my great grandfather on the back porch. He sat in his well-padded wicker chair that gave him a fish eye view of the plains that bordered the mountains. I sat in my wicker chair opposite him. I liked looking at his face as he spoke, I could see the plains and mountains any old time. My great grandfather was ninety-two years, had the springy step of a fifty-year-old and was, I thought, one of the wisest men on the planet.

"They say that I'm ninety-two. Maybe I am, but maybe I'm older than that."

He spoke slowly and paused when he came to the conclusion of what he wanted to say. When I was a busy headed teenager I used to become a little impatient with these pauses. I wanted him to spit it out, to get on with it! But as I got older I began to accept and enjoy the way he talked. He opened up spaces to allow you the time to think about what he was saying. I got the impression he listened to me the same way, with an unhurried rhythm.

"I'm not a modern Indian, I'm an old Indian, a Lakota Sioux man, as they have named it. When I say 'old', I mean I'm one of those who came from the traditional lifestyle of our people.

Our story has been so distorted and lied about so much, lied about so much."

He never cried the blues, but when he was feeling blue about something that he was talking about, he would repeat the words twice. Or sometimes three times – 'lied about so much."

"As a boy I lived on these plains, in the mountains around us. I will always remember how free I felt, how free our lifestyle was. I spent whole days doing nothing but looking up at the sky. Maybe I was in training to become one of those, whatcha call 'em? Astronomers, or something."

He did stuff like that often, made little jokes with a typically dry punch line. He did it with a completely dead pan expression, the silent laughter was in his eyes.

"But don't misunderstand me, Sam, it wasn't all about cloud gathering. As a boy, maybe eight – ten years or so, I had work to do, responsibilities. My main responsibility was herding my father's horses, he had fifty or so, and they were only one or two generations from being wild. I had to be careful with them. I couldn't beat them into submission, I had to out-horse them."

He kept me in a perpetual smile mode and often tripped me into outright laughter.

"Our semi-wild horses were very smart, not like the horses who were completely domesticated; race horses, carriage horses, draft horses 'n all that. These semi-wild horses my father gave us to herd, me and my two brothers were full of tricks and antics. For example, from time to time, fifteen or twenty of them would decide to rebel. That means that they had decided to do whatever the hell they wanted to do.

They might begin to meander too far away from our teepees, yes, teepees. We lived in real houses then, not these storage box-beehive-chicken coops. They had decided that they were going to 'meander' back out there onto the plains, to be completely free again. We had to stop them. What could we do? Well, grandson, as you know, despite all of your schooling, you know that horses are great herd animals . . . ."

Another smile mode joke – "despite all of your schooling" – I had to remain alert for the way he played on me.

"So, the thing to do was to get into the head of the 'chief herder', that was the leader of the 'rebellion.' I discovered that I could do it in one or two ways – I could follow the herd for a bit, become the leader of the herd and take them back to where we wanted them to be. Or I could use salt or apples as bribes for the herd leader.

That was my method, salt and/or apples. Worked like a charm. We lost a few horses, but we kept a lot under control by giving the herd leader salt and/or apples. The white people used that same method with us, later on, but that's another story altogether.

When I was ten or twelve years old, who knows what year that was? My uncle, not my father, fathers were considered to be too tender-hearted for this, took me into those mountains right there in front of us. My uncle gave me a large knife and a few simple instructions . . . .

'You are the great-great-great-grandson of great men. Stay here, fast, try to communicate with them. Find out who you are. Pray.' That's all my uncle said. My uncle was a very powerful 'man of the herbs,' what many people would call 'a medicine man.'

I was left in the mountain, fortunately it was Spring (or did my uncle plan it that way?) with a large knife and a buffalo hide apron around my waist. 'That was it, Sam, that was it.'"

Seems like he took an extra-long time to get back on track after he finished that sentence.

'That was it.' My uncle told me, as he rode away; 'we will be back for you.' He didn't tell me when he, whoever, would be back for me.

I sat under a tree for a long time, trying to figure out what 'we will be back' meant. Tomorrow? Next week? Next month? Next year?

I knew why I was there, no problem about understanding that. In our old tribal life, a boy, at a certain age, was taken off into the mountain, left there to 'deal with himself,' as many of the Modern People would put it. Some of the Modern People would say -- 'he was left in the wilderness to find himself.'

I would accept the modern version of our spirit quest more than that other stuff."

Great Grandfather could put things in a very conclusive way: 'that other stuff.'

"So, I'm left in the mountains with a knife and a buffalo hide apron. Instructed to find out who I am. No food. Even if I had to find and kill something, I was not supposed to eat it. 'Drink water, if you can find it.' That was another one of the things my uncle had said to me. 'Drink water, if you can find it.' That was not going to be a great problem, there were many water sources in those mountains. But if I didn't eat anything I would starve to death. Unless my uncle came to take me back. I became one lonely Injun."

I had to double check what I had just heard – 'one lonely Injun?'

'Yeah, Sam, one lonely Injun. Don't trip out on the term, it just means, nobody else in the world but me.'

I looked from my great Grandfather's face to the mountains behind me. I thought about what it would feel like to spend days and nights up there. There were lots of bears, wolves, coyotes, mountain lions, animals that could eat you up back then. And it is cold at night in the mountains, even in the summer time. He smiled at me, obviously reading my thoughts.

'O yeahhh, it does get cold up there at night, even in the summer time, as you well know.'

My great Grandfather had often taken me for overnight hikes in the mountains. They were always great times for me, with Gramma's fried chicken, biscuits, lemonade and, of course we had sleeping bags. He could identify hundreds of plants and tell me what they could be used for. But the idea of being in the mountains without any clothes on, other than a buffalo hide apron, and only a knife for protection against bears or whatever made me shiver to think about it. I had to ask; 'how long were you going to be up there?'

"When my uncle left me he told me, 'we will be back for you.' He didn't leave me with a time frame. He just told me to fast and pray. And that is what I did. I think the first two days and nights were very hard. And then it got harder. I made my fire the first night, using a hand driven bow drill, a piece of wood and dry moss. That was no big problem.

Strangely, maybe, was the problem of being completely alone, away from those who spoke the language. Understand what I'm saying? There were creatures all around me, exchanging feelings about different things, expressing themselves. I cannot think of a sound that is as deep and beautiful as the sound of a pack of wolves howling to each other. I listened closely to that symphony."

I thought he was going to cry for a minute, something I had only seen him do once in my life. The first and only time happened when 'Snake

Nose,' his favorite horse broke both front legs in gopher holes and had to be put down. The moment passed.

"Up there, in the mountains, I became closer to everything. I prayed to the Great Spirit in the morning, sometimes in the afternoon and, on my second night, I prayed all night. I couldn't help myself, I can't say what my prayers were because that has always been a private matter with me. On the third day I developed a powerful urge to eat something. I watched birds gorge on berries, tart, Spring fresh. I came to a little clearing and found two new born fawns, completely quiet and still, the way their mother had taught them to be since they were born. I had my knife, I could've cut their throats and had tender Spring fawn meat to eat. But I didn't do that. I stepped back a few steps and knelt on the Earth and thanked the Great Spirit for making it possible for me to be so close to my family in the forest.

The doe stepped into the clearing like a little ballerina, paused to study this strange creature kneeling so close to her babies, nudged them to follow her and disappeared into the green curtain/ wall behind her. A second later, she peeked thru the curtain/wall and winked at me. That made me feel very good.

I felt even better that evening, after I had drank a lot of water from the little spring I discovered . . . ."

"The little spring you showed me the first time we went hiking?:

"That's the one. The one I drank from when I was a boy."

He settled back in his chair and let me absorb that thought for a long moment.

"That little spring has always been there, will always be there as long as we keep it a secret." He winked with his left eye.

"You know, grandson, there are no boy who are asked to find something out about themselves these days." Was he changing the narrative? I sat up a little straighter.

"Back then, in that place, at that time, I was being given the opportunity to find out something about myself. On the fourth day, while I was standing there, praying, my eyes closed, my arms open to receive the blessings of the Great Spirit, I felt as though a giant hand had placed me in a canoe and I was being swept along, going up a gently flowing river."

I could feel the moment, I was riding in that canoe with him, with my great Grandfather's spirit.

"Some people might say that I was hallucinating from hunger. No, this was not hallucination from hunger. As a matter of fact, I didn't feel hungry at all . . . ."

"Your body was feeding on itself, consuming its fat reserves."

"I guess that might be one way to look at it . . . ."

I felt a little stupid for coming up with such a numbskull explanation.

"But there was something else happening too. I was being taken to a place filled with hundreds of plants, maybe thousands, and they all seemed to be speaking to me at the same time. I had never thought of plants speaking before. Coyotes, bears, birds, buffalo, but never plants.

The plants were gently hushed by a gentle, warm, wind blowing over them. The wind seemed to be saying – "easy now, easy, one at a time."

I watched as my great Grandfather gracefully eased up out of his chair. Was this the end of the story?

"Gotta go take a leak," he said, with a smile in each corner of his mouth. I was still smiling when he had slid back into his chair, mumbling . . . .. "Ol' man have to pee a lot. Now, where was I?"

"You were somewhere with a lot of plants talking to you."

He nodded in agreement, as though to say . . . good you're still with me. And sat very still, with his eyes closed. I thought he had decided to nap out on me. After a couple full pregnant minutes, he started to speak as his eyes opened slowly. I think I may have reacted with a little shock. His eyes were glazed over, like marbles. And his voice had changed, his voice kept changing with every other sentence, every other sentence for about two hours.

I would never, ever be able to imitate what he said, or the way he said it. But it became clear, after I listened closely, that he was repeating what the plants had told him, in Lakota and English. "When the bee sting, rub me on. Do it few times and everything will be fine."

"I can control the fever, make a tea of my leaves, take it while it's hot."

"The baby is sick with colic, use me, I will be gentle."

"The warrior has been wounded with an arrow, use the juice from my leaves to fight the infection. And tell him to stop fighting."

Like I said, for about two solid hours I listened to the voices that came out of his throat. I was mesmerized, that's the only word I can use to describe what I felt. Gradually, the glazed eyes returned to their normal bloodshot state, like someone who had looked in his own voice, a gravelly baritone.

"So, grandson, you see, the plants, the herbs claimed me up there. They become my friends, my allies, my medicine. I became what many would call a 'medicine man.'"

"How long were you there, in that place with the plants, the herbs?"

"My uncle and my father came for me after nine days, but truth is that I have never left that sacred place I was taken to by the Great Spirit. My father gave me two beautiful horses and my uncle gave me a beautifully made bow, with quail feather tipped arrows. I rode the horses, but I never used the bow and arrows to kill anything. From the time of my days and nights in the mountains I have never eaten meat.

Some thought it was a bit unusual that I no longer had the desire to eat the liver of a fresh killed buffalo, to eat the good deer meat, to feast on the pemmican that the women made for the cold times. Some thought it was unusual, but no one bugged me. They understood where I was coming from. And from that time to this time I have always had people coming to me for cures, for solutions to their problems."

"You once told me that this was the way you learned English. Tell me that story again, I've almost forgotten the details."

He leaned over and gave me a playful punch on my left shoulder. It was a playful punch, but his fist felt like a brick.

"Sam. You are a rascal, you know that? I'll tell you the story again, but before I start, go and get us a couple lemonades, my mouth is dry as a bone."

Gramma was in the kitchen doing something. She was always doing <u>something</u>. She leaned over and offered her right cheek for a grandson kiss.

"You want lemonade? I'll bring it. Is that ol' man wearin' you out with his stories?"

"That ol' man," she called him, with a huge smile on her wide, beige skinned face. Gramma looked almost Asian to me and, and at the age of what? Seventy? Eighty? Her beauty was almost an aura. Nothing physical, it went deeper than that.

They often joked about their courtship, about how they got together, got married.

"This ol'man cornered me in the woods one day whilst I was washin' my body. He just started playin' on his courtship flute, that's what young men did back then, they played music for the girl that they desired. That was the beginning. I was naked in the stream, with my clothes on the bank, so I had to listen. I liked his music. And my father approved of him. That was a very important thing. Then was then."

She followed me onto the porch with a frosted pitcher of her tart flavored lemonade ("I don't use nothin' but honey") and three glasses.

She poured the lemonade into the glasses and before either one took a sip, they quickly dipped their forefingers into their glasses and flicked a few droplets of the liquid onto the floor.

It wasn't the first time I had noticed that they seemed to have a ritual motion for everything. Gramma met the sunrise every day with a prayer of thanksgiving. I grew to understand that this was the Real Thanksgiving, not that other stuff.

A few flickered droplets of lemonade, a few mumbled words in Lakota, and we were good to go. Gramma slid into the padded chair next to her husband and picked up her knitting needles. I hadn't noticed her materials in the chair before she sat down. She started knitting. I had no idea what she was knitting, but she was, as usual, doing <u>something</u>.

"It was a very difficult time, grandson, a very, very difficult time that I'm talking about now. The Ghost Dancers had been shot down like dogs. Wovoka had provoked the Wasichus to kill us because he had visited God, the Most High, and God had given him a few suggestions: go back, Wovoka, clean up your act and the Wasichus will fall into the Earth like dolls.

That didn't happen. The Ghost Dancers were shot because they were dancing for a brighter Native American future. Sounds like the Black Lives Movement, doesn't it?"

He was always tripping me out by connecting dots that my computer ridden mind failed to consider.

"I was just a boy when the Ghost Dancers were killed, when the movement was destroyed. Well, I should say, mostly destroyed, because there were people who continued to dance in secret, underground, so to speak. I'm sure that there are still Dancers out there, somewhere, right now.

Like I said, it was a very difficult time. The People and the Wasichus were bumping heads. I was a boy, hanging around on the fringe of things, but there were two things that became clear to me early on. I could see that the Wasichus didn't understand us and didn't want to understand us. We tried very hard to understand them; I listed to conversations amongst our people, but the consensus, as much as I hate to say it, is that trying to understand the Wasichus's mind was like trying to understand the mind of a mad man. I heard people say, "he kills the buffalo for pleasure, not to feed his family."

It was unbelievable to the People that any human being would kill off the food supply of other human beings. We just couldn't bring ourselves to understand that. Like I said, I was a boy, hanging on the fringes of things. But one thing became quite clear to me. Listening to the exchanges between the People and the Wasichus. The exchanges were taking place with the help of translators/interpreters . . . ."

A cellphone ringing interrupted him. Gramma pulled the phone from her apron pocket and whispered – "I'll call you back later."

"These translators/interpreter were supposed to be the bridge between us and them. Maybe there were a few who really tried to bridge the gap, but I didn't have much respect for most of them. Some of them were drunk, most took the Wasichu point of view, no matter how unfair it was. I didn't have to understand all of the words, I could see the effects.

Early on, as a boy on the fringe, I felt that I could be of great help to our people if I could learn the Wasichu language. But where could I go to do this? I prayed on this matter for a long time."

He paused for a long sip of lemonade.

"You know the old saying? – "When the student is ready, the teacher will appear" – that's what happened to me. There was this Wasichu named McKenzie, a fur trapper, who had married one of our women, a woman named Strong Heart Flower. You remember her, Lisa?"

My Gramma's name was Lisa Fox Tail ("because she is pretty, like the tail of a fox"), but I can only remember Grandfather calling her "Lisa," all the rest of us caller her "Gramma."

"Strong Heart Flower, O yes, she was a bold spirit. It took a lot of nerve to marry a white man, back in those days."

"And I think it took a lot of nerve to marry an Indian woman, and come to live with her relatives. That's what he did. I have to admit that we didn't like him very much, at first. Some of us didn't like him because he was the same color as those who were putting so much on us. Other's didn't like him because they thought of him as a kind of spy in our midst.

All had to cut him some slack after he had been allowed to speak at a few Council meetings. He offered a number of reasonable suggestions about how to deal with his own people.

"You must not try to defeat them by force of arms alone, they are better armed and they outnumber you, my brothers, by the thousands. In order to deal with them, you must use your head more than your arms."

It took a while before he became a trusted member of our Council, but he hung in there. He showed us that some of the Wasichus were good. I saw my opportunity to learn English rise up in front of me in the form of a plant, a man from Scotland ("the Scots are like one of the tribes living in the U.K., like the Welsh and the Irish").

I had no real understanding of what a Scotchman was, or a Welshman, or an Irishman. But Mr. McKenzie spoke English and that's what I wanted to learn. I offered him two horses to teach me English. He laughed 'til tears came to his eyes.

"I'm not the proper fellow to teach you, lad, I barely know the alphabet myself. And I would never accept two horses to teach you."

I thought he was bargaining with me about the acceptance of two horses as a language class fee. I upped my offer to three horses, then four, then five. He stopped laughing,

"O, so you're really serious, eh?"

Our classes started immediately. He was just an average person, not a professor or anything like that, so I guess his way of doing things was a bit unusual. We made an agreement to get together for at least two hours every day, every day. Sometime I would get up at four in the morning to be with him when he went up into the mountains to check his traps.

In the beginning, for the two hours or more that we spent together, he would only speak to me in English . . . ."

Gramma bent over in her chair, laughing like I had never heard her laugh. What was the joke? Grandfather started laughing too. Was this contagious? Gramma recovered from her laugh fit first.

"Grandson, you know why we laugh?"

"I have to confess, I don't have a clue."

"Well, let me tell you." Gramma could "story talk" too, in her own way.

"This good white man, McKenzie, was a Scotch. None of the People really knew what the difference was between the Scotch, the Weesh . . . ."

"Welsh," he corrected her with a big smile.

"O.k., smarty pants, Weelsh, and Irish. They were all Wasichus to the People. So, here is this ol' man learning his English from a Scotch, who spoke the English like he was rolling pebbles in his mouth. Speak like he taught you, sweetie."

My great grandfather leaned back in his chair, held his head in his plant/herb callused hands, as though he was trying to remember something, before this rich Scots brogue came up out of him.

"Gud morrrrning, Surrrr, 'n how're ya this foine morrrrning?"

"This is the way this ol' man was speaking English when he first started playing his flute for me . . . ."

I started laughing myself. I could just see the whole scene; a serious young medicine man, a Lakota brave, speaking Scotch accented English. That would have to be funny.

"Of course," my great grandfather continued, "I didn't continue to lean so hard on my r's after I discovered the difference between Scotch English and Conventional English. In addition to everything else, I had learned enough to know when and how our people were being scalped."

The smiles, the contagious laughter simply dissolved. It felt as though someone had literally tossed a soaking wet, skunk stinking blanket on top of the space we were in, out on the back porch.

I think that Gramma led us out of this place by picking up her knitting and excusing herself.

"That was my sister Rose, she was callin' to ask if I was goin' to church with her tomorrow . . . ."

My great Grandfather could say so much with the slight shake of a pig tailed head, the slow closing and opening of his eyes, the way he folded his hands in his lap.

"Sister Rose, grandson, has been calling my wife for the past thirty-two years, ever since the Mormons climbed into her mind;" Great Grandfather could be a cold dude, when he felt the circumstances determined it.

"Sister Rose is good woman, you understand? Don't get me wrong. I'm not saying that she is a bad person, or that she is proposing that we do bad things. But, what I have said to her and others like her, do not try to expose us to all of the negative spiritual shit that the Wasichus have squatted on your spirit.

This spiritual shit that they regurgitate is so weird that it makes me think of someone who has lost his mind, and his soul. When Sister Rose called one day, after she had been sufficiently brainwashed by the descendants of the Wasichus who had destroyed our food supply, the buffalo, who had herded us off onto reservations for fighting back, Lord praise Crazy Horse! Who had raped our women, cutting their breasts off to make purses, who had tried to turn us into hunted beasts. Let me stop before I throw up. . . .

I asked Sister Rose – "Sister, are you crazy or something? You want us to join the stuff that has done everything it could do to snuff us off the Earth? You want us to be a part of that?

She gives some kind of answer, always. It's like talking to a maniac with some kind of mis-wired brain. She doesn't hear me, or she has been so mis-wired that she can't hear."

"So, grandson, when I receive the call from Sister Rose, I say – "I will call you back later."

The sun was settling behind the mountains, it was time for me to get to the ulterior reason for my visit with my great Grandfather . . . .

"Great grandfather," I never called him, 'Great Grandfather', after he had told me, 'hey, one grandfather is enough, I don't need to be reminded of how old I am. I'm old enough as a grandfather, let's stay with that.'"

"Grandfather, I want to do a spirit quest. Will you help me?"

"Of course I will, grandson, isn't that what you came to ask me?"

XXX    XXX

# CHAPTER 13

"Jonathan, Daniel, we've just finished reading this, what would you call it? A query letter? A first chapter? In any case, it's from one of your former classmates, Sam Young Hawk, and we're going to publish 'From my Great Grandfather's Eyes.' It's a compelling story."

"Sam Young Hawk? I haven't heard or seen that guy in years, he was always disappearing up in the hills for weeks at a time when we were in SoHMAA together. No one could really say anything to him about his habits because he knew more about herbs than all of us put together."

"Well, we can tell you without hesitation that Kosmic Muffin is going to publish 'From My Great Grandfather's Eyes.;"

"That's great . . . ."

"Oh, how's it going with 'Needles, Cupping, Herbs, etc.' . . . ?"

Uhhh, well, you know how it goes, sometimes smooth, sometimes rough . . . ."

CoCo shook her head and smiled. These guys were so secretive, so into what they were doing that they had stopped sharing their pages with their wives.

"C'mon, CoCo, Verona, you guys are publishers now, we should wait 'til we have a finished product to present to you."

Their third novel, "Needles, Cupping, Herbs, etc.," was a satirical look behind the scenes in an "alternative healer's" office. Verona and CoCo cautioned them; "from what we've read thus far, you guys are going to piss off a lot of 'alternative' practitioners."

"And so what?" They chorused in response. And it was on.

XXX     XXX

"Ancestral Meridians"

"Internal Discussions"

"From my Great Grandfather's Eyes"

"Needles, Cupping, Herbs, etc."

"Verona, doesn't it give you a kick just to say the titles that we, that Kosmic Muffin has released?"

"You better believe it. And don't forget Krystal's translation of 'Ancestral Meridians.' I'm glad we decided to do the printing and release right here in the good ol' U.S. of A."

"Who needs more outsourcing?"

They took simultaneous sips of their espresso. Another Saturday meeting at the Café Oro.

"Oh, incidentally, while we're sitting here patting ourselves on the back about our smooth operation, I think this is as good a time as any to talk about this bump in the road that was delivered to the office yesterday."

Verona slid a large, official looking envelope across the table to her friend/co-publisher.

"What's this? Another piece of bureaucratic nonsense?"

"I guess you say that, in a way."

Coco's look of curiosity changed to jaw dropping surprise as she read page after page of legalese.

"This is unbelievable, can she actually do this?"

"She can certainly try. Mrs. Stella-ex-wife-of-the man once known as Robert 'Bob' Bradford, is bringing a suit against Kosmic Muffin Publishing, because she feels that we owe her something. I have to say, as a lawyer, that she is definitely making an unreasonable demand, and we will not have a hard time beating her in a court of law."

"I don't doubt that, but what in the world would make her come out of the wood pile after all these years?"

"It's called greed, my friend, simply greed. Aside from everything else, it establishes our place in the publishing world . . . ."

"How's that?"

"As one of my lawyer pals once said, 'You're not really in the public eye 'til you've been sued.'"

They high fived and signaled the waiter for two more cups of nerve juggling caffeine.

XXX    XXX

CoCo read the first fifty pages of Nelson Wang's autobiographical novel for the second time. It seemed to be worse the second time around. She looked up from the neatly arranged desk to stare out of the window that framed their brown shaded fall garden.

The works slid though her mind, a roller coaster going up and up: "Ancestral Meridians," a bit spooky, but interesting stuff to read. The "Box Brown" work. "The Emperor's Needles," they had casually nicknamed Daniel's story about the discovery of the golden needles. "From my Great Grandfather's Eyes," Sam Young Hawk's beautiful story of his relationship to his great grandfather and how it felt, what happened to him when he went to the mountains to experience what his spirit had in store for him. A gorgeous narrative. "Internal Discussions," a satirical look at the "Alternative" medical field.

"You guys are going to piss off a lot of 'alternative' practitioners."

"And so what?" They chorused in response. And it was on. "'Needles, Cupping, Herbs, etc.' Another satire. If 'Internal Discussions' didn't piss 'em off, then surely 'Needles' will do the trick."

"Dan, Jonathan, are you guys trying to deliberately antagonize anybody?"

"Not really. We're simply saying, if you want to look at it this way – you can be a vegan and have a sense of humor too. You know what I'm saying?"

"Yeah, Dan, I know what you're saying."

Her desk phone ringing jarred her from her roller coaster/random thoughts.

"Good afternoon, Kosmic Muffin Publishing . . . ."

"Sounds good, CoCo, sounds good. . . ."

"O hi, Verona, what's up?"

"I'll give you an update on the latest suit in a minute – have you had a chance to read the Wang manuscript?" CoCo closed her eyes and tried to wish the question away. Verona pulled up on the hesitant vibe.

"Uhhh, CoCo, you still there?"

"Yeah, Verona, I'm still here. And yes, yes, I've just finished reading the first fifty pages of 'The Chinese Guy.'"

"You don't sound very enthusiastic."

"Have you read it?"

"Just a few pages. I don't like the title very much."

"And if you read the first fifty pages you wouldn't like them either. I'm sure that Nelson Wang is a fine doctor, but he's not a very fine writer."

"Ooohh no, what a disappointment. Remember how pleased Dan and Jonathan were when we told them about another ol' classmate submitting a manuscript to Kosmic Muffin? What's the biggest problem with the work?"

"Honestly, the biggest problem is the work itself. The writing is like a doctor writing a prescription. Once he gets past – 'all through high school my classmates referred to me as 'the Chinese Guy.' Maybe it had something to do with the fact that my grandparents had immigrated here from a small village in China . . . .' it slides downhill with remarkable speed. He has no sense of story, let's say, like Jonathan, Daniel or Sam Young Hawk. "I had to force myself to read the glacial sentences, his attempts to be witty --- no one seemed to laugh at my jokes, they just frowned."

"That bad, huh?:

"Verona, read my lips – Nelson Wang is not a writer. Maybe he spent too many hours writing memos or something, I can't say. What I can say is this, it would not be a good idea for the Kosmic Muffin Publishing House to publish 'The Chinese Guy.'"

"I know you're right, but I feel really bad about this, our first rejection."

"Moving right along. What's the latest suit about?"

"Here's the deal. It seems that some descendants of Mr. Henry 'Box' Brown. . . ."

"Descendants of Mr. Henry 'Box' Brown, a runaway gentleman from the great state of Virginia to the great state of Pennsylvania?"

"One and the same. These alleged descendants are suing the Kosmic Muffin Publishing House . . . ."

"For what?"

"Well, CoCo, to keep the brief brief, they're asking for some of the money that Kosmic Muffin might earn from the residuals of the sales of 'Out of the Box, the Helen B. Brown Story.'"

"So, what're we going to do about this?"

"It's already been done. I contacted Henry Brown at his home in Copenhagen, explained the situation to him and he solved the problem in about five minutes. He suggested that we, Kosmic Muffin Publishing House, should establish a Henry 'Box' Brown Fund/Foundation that would do several things. For those people of college age who could pass a 'Box' DNA test, they would be able to apply for scholarships.

For senior citizens who could offer verifiable DNA proof, financial aid would be available. Now then, for those who are in between those two demographics, we just might send them a percentage of the profits, after our operating costs have been dealt with."

"Sounds great. I really like that DNA part, it means that we can cut away a lot of 'great pretenders' right at the beginning."

"You got that right. In addition Mr. Brown suggested that we allow this suit an opportunity to be taken to court. He thinks it might offer a wonderful p.r. moment. I thought about it for a bit and I think he's completely right. It'll be great publicity for the Henry 'Box' Brown lobby, for Kosmic, and the people who claim legitimate descent from that incredible human being who was brave enough to escape chattel slavery, nailed inside a dry good box."

"My claustrophobia kicks in every time I think about that 30- hour torture chamber trip."

"You too? I know I would never have made it. So, there it is. There are a few kinks that we might have to work out, but I think his suggestions are right on the money."

"No doubt in my mind. Sounds like the Henry 'Box' Brown thing is going to offer us some very positive results. Now then, going back to Dr. Nelson Wang's awful manuscript, you know we don't even have 'rejection notices' on hand."

"Couldn't you e-mail him?"

"Is that the way it's done?"

"I don't know, I've never given anybody a rejection notice."

There was a very pregnant pause before CoCo booted up.

"Verona, I have a good idea. Why don't you invite Dr. Wang for lunch at that Vietnamese restaurant over there in Long Beach? You know, pay for the guy's lunch and then crack him over the head with the bad news."

"CoCo, you're a literary coward . . . ."

"I know. And I'm not ashamed. Why don't both of us meet with him?"

"I'm just as much a coward as you are, but we have to do what we have to do. Good idea, both of us can hurt him together."

The meeting was scheduled, they had a delicious lunch and forced themselves to tell Dr. Nelson Wang that his manuscript was not up to Kosmic Muffin's standards.

"Well, as you can see, from my manuscript, I'm not the greatest writer who ever used an acupuncture needle."

They were on the verge of tears when they got in their cars. It was an awful thing, they both felt, to reject someone. Dr. Wang didn't seem to look at it that way.

"Maybe next time, huh? And even if you reject me, I'll get a delicious Vietnamese lunch out of it."

XXX    XXX

## Two Pearls

By Anouska Mehta

"I think it would be proper for me to say a few words about myself before I attempt to say a few words about others. The others, in this case being Jewel Pearl Williams and Acanit Bigombe. I am the oldest of two children. Brother Sanjay is two years younger. We were, when we lived there, one of the high caste Brahmin families in Benares, one of the great holy cities in India. It always pains me a bit when I have to say 'high caste,' but I must face reality and state the truth. The reason I am making this statement will be explained later in this narrative.

As a child, like most children, I had no particular sense of being an Indian in India. I was simply happy to be doing whatever I was doing. I was in a state of innocence. Our family was affluent, which meant that we had everything we wanted. How old was I? Five? Six? Maybe seven, when I first became aware of certain things.

For example, I noticed, when our chauffeur drove us through the narrow streets of Benares, that there were people living on the streets. Yes, literally living on the streets, like people in Los Angeles, New York, Chicago. I can't say why, at this late date, why the sight of those people on the streets made such a great impact on me.

Several other things touched me also. One afternoon my father was walking through a narrow lane with me and my brother, perhaps we were going to buy sweets from our local sweet shop. Indians love their sweets.

Suddenly, my father, who was usually a very calm person, became quite agitated. He actually screamed at a man who was approaching us from the opposite end of the lane – 'Go back! Go back, you imbecile! Your shadow is about to fall on us!'

The man, obviously a poor person from the way he was dressed, hung his head in a shameful way and quickly turned around and ran in the direction he had come from.

My father stood in place, literally seething with anger. 'They know they're not supposed to use this lane,' he mumbled to himself.

My brother and I exchanged puzzled expressions. What was going on here?

'Come,' he said to us, 'we will go through another lane, this one is polluted.'

We made a wide detour to get to our sweet shop. It wasn't 'til later that day, when my father and mother were having tea, did I begin to have an inkling of an understanding of what Sanjay and I had witnessed.

'He was walking through the lane as though he felt he belonged there.'

'Some of them have become quite cheeky,' Mother commented as she sipped her tea.

'I'm afraid I will have to have the proper ceremonies performed, to make certain that the pollution is cleared.' Mother nodded in agreement. I simply felt confused. As a 'precocious imp,' my mother used to call me with affection, I was determined to find out what this was all about. The person to go to? My father's chauffeur-valet-fetch go man, Mr. Ghosh. I found him polishing our already shiny automobile.

I tumbled in on him, the way privileged children are apt to do all over the world, giving the poor man a kiddie description of what had happened, and asking for an explanation that would make sense to me. Mr. Ghosh was a plain spoken person, not given to dramatic pauses and so on.

'The person who caused the master so much distress was an Untouchable. Mahatma Gandhi gave them some other name, and they may call themselves something else, but <u>we</u> know who they are and <u>they</u> know who they are.'

'You mean that they are people who can't be touched? And how could they pollute my father?'

Mr. Gosh frowned and began to polish the shiny car again.

'You must speak with your father these matters, I am not the person you should speak with.'

I couldn't take Mr. Ghosh's advice because I just didn't feel that I should question my father about this. My brother Sanjay supplied an answer, of sorts, within a month or so later.

'I found out why Father was so upset about that man in the lane.'

'Why?'

'Because he is an Untouchable and we are Brahmins.'

"So what does that mean?'

Sanjay stared at me in a very peculiar way. He resembled my father, 'specially the eyes and nose.

'That means that he is a very low caste person and we are very high caste. And we have to be careful to keep our distance from them.'

'Because their shadows could 'pollute' us?'

'Yes, even their shadows.'

'Rubbish!'

Sanjay had no problem with the caste system but it tortured my soul, even as a young girl. Another deeply impacting thing happened to me when I was about twelve or so, going to this very posh private school. One day, walking across our neatly manicured campus, I came across a small clump of girls staring at something behind their hands. I maneuvered my way into the group to see what they were looking at, what they were giggling about.

About twenty yards in front of us was a sewage manhole, one of those small cart with a donkey, the kind they use all over rural India, with a large metal barrel in the cart. Is that what the girls were giggling about?

No, it wasn't that, it was the sight of a slender young man climbing up out of the manhole with a huge bucket of feces on his back. He was a member of the shit caste, doing his job, and the upper caste girls were making fun of him. I felt sorry for him. The shit sloshed down his face and back, the stench carried over to us. So, this is why they were giggling behind their hands.

131

The sun was fierce, his work seemed unbearable. I pulled a plastic bottle of water out of my back pack and threw it within easy reach of his filthy hands. He dumped his load into the barrel, climbed down off the back of the cart and stared at the bottle of water. The numb expression didn't change, he didn't look around to see who had offered him water, he simply picked it up and climbed back down into the sewer. I like to think that the water tasted delicious to him, despite the shit.

I caught holy hell for my act of kindness, starting with the Head Mistress and ending with my father.

'My dear,' was the way father started his lecture to me. 'My dear' was an expression he used when he was really angry with me. Hearing him say, 'my dear,' was like feeling an ice pick plunge into my heart. I sat on an ottoman in front of his favorite leather bound chair.

'My dear, Mrs. Bhayani has informed us of your outrageous conduct this afternoon . . . .'

'Father, all I did was give a thirsty man some water.'

I had to be careful with what I said, after all, a Father is a Father in India, and one must show respect.

'We're not sending you to the Divakruni School for Girls in order for you to try to reform our society. We are sending you to this school in order for you to know how to take your proper place in our society. Are you listening to me, my dear?'

'Yes, Father, I'm listening . . . ."

'What I must make you understand is actually quite simple; we were born to be a certain way, to fulfill certain functions in this life, all of us, from the very lowest to the very highest. Are you listening to me, my dear? We cannot make ourselves responsible for what God has decided.'

I had no choice but to nod in agreement. Who could argue about what God has decided? Or what my Father said God had decided. I nodded in agreement but I didn't believe what my Father said. I felt empowered to know that I could rebel mentally, without exposing myself. It made me feel good.

'India is a great country, my dear, a great country. And it would be greater now if we had been able to keep the English out of here.'

Father's lecture lasted for thirty-five minutes and covered many different areas. One of his strongest points concerned his attitude about education for girls/women

'If I had listened to members of my family, friends, and others, you would not be in school now. I've resisted their advice to keep you out of school. You should be grateful, my dear.'

'I thank you, Father.' I told him and kissed his feet."

XXX    XXX

# CHAPTER 14

I SUFFERED A LOT AFTER that lecture from my father. In some strange way, it seemed to make me feel more conscious of unfair treatment, starting in our own household. I saw mother push and slap the girls, maids who served us, whenever she wasn't pleased with them. Father often spoke rudely to Mr. Ghosh and the others in our household.

And on several occasions I saw one of the maids leave Sanjay's room in tears. What was going on? I caught her in the lower corridor and asked – "Swathi, what happened? Why are you crying?"

She looked up at me, a girl about my own age, her big eyes brimming with tears. Before she could say anything, Sanjay leaned over the upstairs bannister and called down to me.

"Leave her go! This is no concern of yours!"

I was surprised to hear my brother speak so rudely to me and I hate to admit, even now, that I was so naïve, so sexually unsophisticated, that I had no idea what was happening. I must say, in those days, mothers didn't talk to their daughters about the sexual realities of the world. I don't think many people put two and two together, concerning sexual harassment/exploitation until women began to speak openly about rape. There is still a great deal of resistance even in this day and age, to the idea of treating women fairly and equally. I was fifteen years old when my mother came to tell me that she and my father had 'negotiated' a very good marriage for me with an outstanding young man from a high caste family. The outstanding 'young man' was only thirty-six years old. My father explained.

"His first wife was killed in a train accident six years ago. He is a professional man, an architect, and he is not asking for a great dowry.

Aside from everything else he has agreed to allow you to continue to go to school, that is, until you become pregnant."

I cried all night for three days. I didn't want to be married to anyone, especially to a 'young man' of thirty-six. My weeping didn't matter. A great colorful ceremony was performed and suddenly, it seemed to me, I was the virgin bride of a man named Zubin Mehta. I had the feeling that my parents had married me off because I was beginning to be a pain the neck for them. I cannot say that that was the absolute truth, or just my injured feelings.

So far as I was concerned the marriage was an absolute disaster from the first night we got into the same bed together. It wasn't difficult for my mother to show my in-laws the blood stained sheet, the physical evidence of their daughter's virginity, because my husband's physical attack had made me bleed. Such pain. No one had talked to me about sex, about what a husband and a wife did together. My husband pulled my legs apart, pushed himself inside of me, hard, grunted like a bull a few times, and rolled down to 'his side' of the bed and started snoring.

I can remember laying there, feeling violated. Somewhere, in my readings, I had read of something called "love making." Was this "love making?" If it was, I didn't want to have anything to do with it. My feelings didn't matter. I was a married woman now, a wife, and a wife's first consideration was her husband's feelings.

Fortunately, my husband was a senior partner in the architectural firm of Chopra, Jain and Mehta, which meant that he didn't have a lot of time to practice his assaults on my body. That's what it was for me, an assault on my body. He came home from his work, he ate his dinner, had a few drinks of Scotch, assaulted me and went to sleep.

I learned how to disassociate my mind from what was happening. While he was grunting, enjoying what he was doing, I was busy re-writing my essay on "The Problems of the British Middle Class," or whatever.

One night he slapped me on the side of my face and growled like an animal; "you're not with me."

"With you where?" I asked, not knowing what he meant.

Our relationship was not good, but my relationship with my in-laws, especially my mother-in-law was even worse. This woman hated me, made life completely miserable for me (I was moved into my in-laws home when

Zubin and I got married, as was the custom) by doing and saying all sorts of mean spirited things.

"Why are you so dark, did your mother have a nightmare before you were born?"

In the beginning, before I developed a thick skin, I was completely devastated by comments like that. Of course I could've replied with more sarcasm than this short, heavy set toad would've been able to deal with, but I couldn't do that, I would be insulting my husband's mother, a big No No."

[A word or two about color in India. Lighter skinned women are preferred over darker skinned women, especially in the higher classes/castes. There are many reasons whys this is so; one of the major reasons is that there is an assumption that the lighter skinned individual is the descendant of "superior people."]

I think, in order to place a buffer between me and my toad-witch mother-in-law, and my husband's "love making," I made a subconscious effort to excel in my studies.

Headmistress Bhayani even acknowledged my superior work – "Anouska, you are not doing badly, you will definitely be ready for university after your last term of Divakruni. I offer my congratulations on your work ethic, I wish all of our girls had your talent and drive. And you, a married woman!"

University? I had not allowed myself to think that far ahead. I tried to talk with my husband about the matter, but he was dismissive.

"You don't need to go to University, you need to settle down and become my wife, and a good mother." That was it, so far as he was concerned – "my wife and a good mother."

I was so depressed I thought about suicide, yes, I thought about killing myself. I was swamped by all of the stuff I was dealing with. My life was saved, literally by one of my classmates, one of my classmates who was also married.

"Anouska, your husband has said that you can go to school until you are pregnant? Right?"

"Yes," I nodded. Zubin had said something to that effect.

"Well," she continued, "do you want to get pregnant so that you won't be able to continue your education?"

"Of course no!"

Aruna, that was my friend's name, dug into her back pack and pulled out a small packet of pills.

"If you use these you won't get pregnant until you are ready."

"What are these?"

"Birth control pills."

I suddenly felt like a weight had been lifted from my head and shoulders. Aruna helped me by giving me some of her pills . . . .

"Don't worry, I have plenty, these should last you until we get your supply."

I was on pins and needles, waiting for a couple days, 'til Aruna arranged for me to make a connection with her supplier. I was afraid that Zubin's almost nightly attacks may have already impregnated me. I got lucky, I managed to purchase a six-month supply of a Swiss brand of birth control pills – "These are the very best"– before I got pregnant.

I had to be very careful. If my husband or my in-laws, meaning my toad faced mother-in-law, found out what I was doing I would be considered a disgrace to my family. And even worse; there were cases where "rebel wives" had been doused with kerosene and set afire. There was a strong feeling against wives who 'betrayed' their in-laws.

I continued doing well in school and badly at home. My mother-in-law began to plant ugly seeds in my husband's mind.

"I think she is barren. You have been married for ten months now and she is not pregnant, she must be barren or else she is using something to prevent herself from becoming pregnant. She is deceiving you, my son, she is deceiving you."

I felt so bad, being forced to lie to my husband, to deceive him, but I had no choice. If I confessed that I <u>had</u> been taking the pill, it would be just as bad as saying that I <u>was</u> taking the pill. I was dammed either way.

I had nothing to do with what happened two days after my husband "interrogated" me. My mother-in-law was literally holding me captive in the kitchen, jumping all over me about my lack of cooking skills.

"It doesn't matter that we have servants, we must still know how to prepare food properly, so that we will know if the servants are doing the proper thing." She emphasized her point by banging me on my knuckles with her wooden spoon.

One of the servants ran into the kitchen – "please come! There has been a terrible accident!" News travels with lightning speed in Benares. Within an hour we were informed that a building designed by the architectural firm of Chopra, Jain and Mehta, had collapsed while my husband was doing an inspection tour of the site, to make certain that the builders were using the correct building materials. Indian contractors had a bad reputation for using substandard building materials.

Zubin was on the fourth floor of the building when it collapsed, killing him and thirty others. The Mehta family went into deep mourning, seeming to forget about me for a few days. I grieved for my husband, like all of the members of his family. I could never say that I loved the man, but I certainly didn't want to see him dead.

XXX     XXX

It took only a few days after Zubin's funeral rite, his cremation, before I realized that my life was in danger. I was a sixteen and a half year old widow. And my mother-in-law hated me. I think she actually believed that I was responsible, somehow, for my husband's death. The tension was very great in the house.

I had no choice but to turn to my Father for help. My Mother and brother had said enough, over the course of the months that I had been married to Zubin, to indicate that they didn't feel sympathetic towards me about anything. Father was my last resort.

"Father, please help me . . . ."

"Yes, I will help you. Don't come here, I will meet you somewhere. And you must not say anything to anyone about my involvement. Is that clear?"

"Yes, Father, and thank you."

Three days later, big black bags under my eyes, half-starved from worry and fear, I boarded a British Airways plane to London. My Father had been informed by "one of his sources" that the Mehta family planned to kill me.

"I cannot believe that they would do such a thing, but I know that it is possible. You have not done anything that entitles them to kill you."

I do believe that they would've doused me with kerosene and set me afire. It happens frequently.

"Remember, Anouska, you must never tell anyone about my involvement, it would completely ruin our family. Is that clear?"

"Yes, Father . . . ."

I felt like a felon fleeing prison. In a way, according to some people, I <u>was</u> a felon. I had committed a crime by not remaining in India, in my in-laws' household, to be treated like a slave. So far as they were concerned I was worthless. What does one do with an overeducated sixteen and a half-year-old widow?

My Father gave me a parting gift of $5,000.00 and a piece of good advice – "continue your education. You are a bright girl and there are many opportunities for women in England. We are planning a trip to London next year, we will see you then." I have never felt so lonely as I felt on that flight from Benares, India to London, England. My Father had helped immensely by giving me money and the addresses and phone numbers of a couple people he knew in London.

"These people can give you a little help, perhaps with finding a room, but don't lean on them, they have their own issues to deal with."

And that's the way it was. I didn't ask for a lot and they didn't offer a lot.

"There is a very nice Irishwoman nearby who will rent you a decent room for a good price."

I got the room and began to try to put my life back together. I spent my first full week in the local library. Headmistress Bhayani had once mentioned something about "The British School." It seems that this was an institution designed to help emigrants from former British colonies acclimate to the English way of life. Their website offered loads of information about grants, funds, scholarships, etc.

On the morning of my appointment I spent twenty minutes trying to decide whether I should wear a sari or a skirt and blouse. I chose the sari. It was more an intuitive decision than anything else.

The office I went to was filled with people from all over the ex-British Empire. I signed a roster and waited my turn. It took them an hour to get to me.

A young Englishman called me to his cubicle, asked a lot of questions as he filled out a form. He stopped in the middle of his questions, stared at me and said; "You are very beautiful." No one had ever told me that I was "beautiful." What reply was I supposed to give?

"You are also beautiful," I replied. I will never forget the huge smile that spread across his face, and the shade of red that spread up from his neck to his forehead. His name was Mr. David Blair and he was <u>very</u> helpful.

"Mrs. Mehta, you are <u>not</u> sixteen going on seventeen, you are eighteen going on nineteen. Isn't that so, Mrs. Mehta?"

As I said, he was <u>very</u> helpful. As a sixteen-year-old I would not have been eligible for anything. It took him exactly two days to find me a job ("not a problem with your excellent English") and steer me into a university program.

"We will have to 'develop' the proper credentials for you because things are always being lost in route from India. Are you getting me, Mrs. Mehta?"

When I think back on it, I have the feeling that I was in a state of grace, a dream state. Case in point: I think David Blair fell in love with me at first sight and knocked himself out doing things for me.

"Anouska, we're upgrading your job status, from an overseas credit marketer to receptionist at the Devonshire Plaza Hotel. Think you can handle it?"

"Yes, David. I think I can handle anything."

I thought, after six months in London, that I <u>could</u> handle anything. The city's demands were relentless. Just using the tube, the underground railroad system was enough of a challenge for any sane person. The biggest problem I faced, that I had a real problem with, was dealing with the helpful Mr. David Blair.

"But Anouska, I love you – why can't we make love?"

"David, I've told you the whole story. My husband was killed, I'm a widow and I shall remain a widow until I re-marry, if ever."

"That means that you won't make love with anyone, that you won't have lovers?"

"Yes, that means exactly that."

"But, but, you are very beautiful."

"And you are also very beautiful," I replied. We laughed at the memory of our first meeting. I couldn't explain what "lovemaking" meant for me. Mr. Zubin Mehta had left a permanent impression on my mind concerning "lovemaking." I didn't want to run the risk of having any more of that, not from an Indian or an Englishman.

XXX    XXX

# CHAPTER 15

It DIDN'T TAKE VERY LONG for India to seem very far away. Of course I missed my family and all that, but I must be honest and say that I didn't miss the desperate poverty of India, the desperate quality of life that so many millions lived with on a daily basis. Yes, there were poor people in London, in England, but I never had the feeling that their situations were hopeless. Maybe it was simply a matter of perception, but I was stuck with it.

The English (thank you, David Blair, "Mr. Beautiful") were friendly and very helpful to me. I know that there are other immigrants who could tell a completely different story. The biggest problem I had with London, with England, was the weather. Yes, the weather. After two years of gray, dim, dismal, damp, cold, rainy weather, I felt desperate to feel the sun on my face again. My opportunity to have the sun on my face occurred as a result of a chance conversation I had with a Chinese-American doctor who was spending a few days at the Devonshire Plaza Hotel. He was on his way back to Santa Monica, USA, from a conference in Beijing.

"I wish we had people as efficient as you are, Ms. Mehta."

"For your organization?"

"Yes, for SoHMAA, we're on our way into our first year."

"Do you think that there would be a place for me if I came there?"

"I can assure you that we would make a place for you."

Dr. Chan was as good as his word. It took me almost a year to get there, but when I arrived there was a welcome mat spread at the front door with my name on it.

XXX    XXX

141

Santa Monica was a section of Heaven after London. Someone had to tell me that we were experiencing a winter rain when it happened.

"But the rain is so warm, like a shower."

They had no idea what a body chilling experience an English winter rain could feel like. SoHMAA was another delightful experience. Everybody knows the story of how a collection of American and Chinese doctors got together to share their medical knowledge. It was considered a wild and radical thing at the time.

It was as though the doctors had decided to say – to hell with petty politics, philosophical differences and all the rest. What we want to do is come together and offer humanity the best possible medical attention they can receive.

I think, even today, that still might be considered a radical concept. I was in the right place at the right time. I started off as a receptionist and, being ambitious, I started to rise. I actually surprised myself to discover that I had an aptitude, a feel for how things could be done in a better way.

I decided to become a social psychologist, majoring in women's studies. It seemed like a natural place for me to go. Three short years later I was voted to become the Director of SoHMAA. I was stunned by my selection. Dr. Chan, the man who had "recruited" me, explained.

"Anouska, we are a young vibrant organization, we don't feel the need to have people with three yard long resumes, twenty years in one spot and all that. We want people like yourself, imaginative, creative, adaptive.

SoHMAA is going to grow and you're going to grow with it."

### XXX     XXX

I was in my third year as Director of SoHMAA and so many things had happened, so many things. But two events stick out in my memory. I have to start with Dr. Jashina Alam becoming a member of our SoHMAA staff. Dr. Jashina Alam from Benares, India, my old home town. And the second event, well, that came a bit later.

Ayurveda! My God! How could we not have Ayurvedic medicine as a central part of our curriculum? And me, an Indian, why didn't I think of it sooner? Ayurveda, a medical tradition that was recorded more than 5,000 years ago in Sanskrit, in the four sacred texts called the Vedas; the

Rig Veda (3000-2500 BCE) Yajur Veda, Sam Veda and Atharva Veda (1000- 1200 BCE)

I suggested that we bring a qualified Ayurveda teacher aboard and received a unanimous vote of yea! In brief, the Ayurvedic theory of "medicine" states that all area of life impact one's health, so it follows that the Vedas cover a wide variety of topics, including health, healthcare techniques, astrology, spirituality, government and politics, art and human behavior. I changed human to humane.

Honestly, I only knew what I knew about Ayurvedic medicine from what I had experienced in my own life, in the home of my parent's and, just to give them their props, in the home of my in-laws. I got busy. I was making a suggestion before fully knowing all I needed to know about the subject, but I got "immediately busy," as one of my students used to say.

We really got lucky by being able to snag Dr. Alam. She had a Ph.D. and all the rest of that, but aside from the academic credentials she was a very wise person. There were other Indians in SoHMAA, but they didn't have the impact on me that she had.

A small, shapely woman, forty-two years old (I had her record), unmarried, her face always smiling or about to smile. We had to tighten the requirements for students wanting to join her class. I wanted to join her class, but I didn't have the time.

I think we sort of circled around each other for the first month she was on campus. She was busy and I was also busy, but then, on a "walk thru" of the campus buildings, something I did as often as I could, I heard the seductive music of the sarod and the tablas. I was on the first floor of the Living Arts building. The music was coming from somewhere. The building was empty, deserted. I think there was a brief recess of some sort.

The tears started as I slowly made my way up to the second floor. I had to pause, to dry my eyes before I made it to the second floor. Why was I crying? The easy answer would be to say that the sound of the sarod and the tablas had made me instantly homesick. But there was more to it than that. I was listening to a music that spoke to me, that said – it's alright to shed tears, it doesn't mean that you are unhappy or happy, it means that the music suggests that you should shed tears. And that's what you are doing. You are Being.

Dr. Jashina Alam was sitting behind her desk. She stood, smiled, offered me a very gracious Namasté, and gestured for me to sit anywhere in the empty classroom. I sat opposite her at her desk, I wanted to look into her face as we listened to our music.

Ali Akbar Khan, Sarod, Alla Rakha, Tabla. Ravi Shankar, Sitar, Zakir Hussain, Tabla. Masters of our musical tradition, a duet for sitar and sarod, a recorded performance from Carnegie Hall – May 5, 1982. Did I mention N.C. Mullick, R.C. Verma and Daniel Karp on tanpuras? How long did we sit there, absorbing the music? I can't say. I do know that the sun was bright and shiny, a typical Santa Monica summer day when I sat to share the music with Dr. Alam, and a golden twilight was washing over us from the western side windows when the music glissed to an end.

There were also a dozen students occupying seats around and behind us.

"I promised them a class this afternoon," she whispered apologetically. There was nothing to say. I returned her smile-Namasté – and continued my academic walk thru. It was a waste of time. What could I discover that Ravi Shankar and Ali Akbar Khan hadn't revealed to me? -- "the rich melodies and rhythm of Indian music reflect every human emotion, every subtle feeling in man/woman/nature that can be musically expressed and experienced." Record liner notes.

Plus; "a raga is the projection of the artist's inner spirit, a manifestation of his most profound feelings and sensibilities. The musician must breathe life into each raga as he unfolds and expands it so that each note shimmers and pulsates with life and the raga is revealed vibrantly and incandescent with beauty." More notes.

That is what the musicians who created this incredible music said. And I had to come all the way to America to pay it any serious attention. God Bless America, if you know what I mean?

I wasn't often exposed to Dr. Alam's "classes" because I wasn't privileged to have the time, but whenever I happened to stumble into her space at the proper time, I was always granted an extraordinary spiritual experience.

It was weeks after my introduction to her "raga feeling" class/lecture, which ended with, typically; "I hope most of you got that?"

Once again I was drawn to the second floor of the Living Arts building. Whoooaa . . . what was I hearing? African music? Dr. Alam welcomed me with a smile and her gracious namasté.

"Dr. Mehta, what you are now hearing is the music of the African-Cuban Masters of percussion – Chano Pozo, Mongo Santamaria, Francisco Aguabella, the inimitable Armando Peraza, the incredibly melodic Carlos 'Patato' Valez, Tata Guinee, David Ponce, Papaito, Julito Collazo, Willie BoBo, Pablo Mozo, Arsenio Rodriguez Machito, Ray Barretto, Jose Mangual, 'Buyu,' I could go on and on abut the African-Cuban masters of musical percussion, but I won't do that. Just allow me to say – there's no musical tradition greater than any other, each has its jewels."

I felt like a piece of Naan being prepared for chewing. And then there was that day I wandered into her classroom. No musical seduction/lure this time. I simply wandered in and we started talking. Incidentally, she was a likely to have her class at the beach as in the classroom.

"Dr. Mehta, that is your married name, is it no?"

I simply nodded yes.

"You husband, Zubin Mehta, the architect was killed in a building accident?"

Once again I nodded yes. Was she doing a psychic reading of my life?

Dr. Alam took a deep breath. Was this the pre-requisite to something else about my past?

"You packed up to London, did what you did there and wound up here, at SoHMAA. Correct?"

Where was all of this leading? I didn't have a good feeling about where this was heading.

"Yes, as you can see, I'm here.:

"When did you last hear from your family?"

I had to think on that question for a moment. Because of what had happened we seldom communicated, and always by e-mail.

"I received an e-mail just last week from my father, he was telling me that the circumstances that caused me to leave Benares, which I don't want to get into, have changed and that I should return home at my earliest available opportunity. Why do you ask that question?"

An uncharacteristic frown gripped Dr. Alam's forehead. I was really puzzled. What's going on here?

"May I ask if your father has sent you similar e-mails in the past?"

"Well, yes, as a matter of fact he has. What're you getting at, Dr. Alam?"

She stared off into the distance for a second or two.

"Dr. Mehta, your father has been dead for at least a year now . . . ."

I stared at her, a cold chill running down my spine. I knew that she would never lie about such a thing.

"Please allow me to explain. Your father's man, Mr. Ghosh, is a cousin of a man who works for our family. As you know, this is one of the ways that news travels so fast in Benares, especially amongst upper caste families. I knew something of the circumstances about your leaving Benares before I met you, the servant to servant news network . . . ."

"Did they know that my father had helped me escape from my in-laws?"

"Yes," she answered without hesitation. "Someone at Barclay's Bank passed the information that your father had withdrawn $5,000.00. It was a simple matter for your in-laws to put two and two together. It also gave them ample opportunity to drag your family's name through the mud. Your father had done a very bad thing, according to our custom, and they made him suffer for it. I cannot say with absolute certainty, but I believe the disgrace may have had been a factor in his death."

"I couldn't stop the slow, thick flow of tears.

"So, my mother and my brother, how did they take this, my father's death?"

I will never forget the pain filled expression that clouded Dr. Alam's normally smiling face.

"Your mother made suttee, committed suicide on your father's funeral fire. No one tried to stop her. And now, so far as I know, your brother goes about the city, drinking alcohol all the time."

The thick flow of tears coated my cheeks.

"Dr. Alam, I don't understand, the e-mails?"

"My guess would be that the e-mails have been sent to you by your in-laws, in an effort to lure you back to Benares so that they can do you harm. Oh, incidentally, to add a bigger reason for them to do you harm, one of your friends, someone named Aruna, confessed that the two of you were sharing birth control pills. That confirmed, to your in-laws, that you are some kind of witch who had something to do with your husband's death."

"O my God no!"

She cradled me in a motherly embrace and allowed me to dampen her shoulder with tears. I've never felt so bad in my whole life.

"Anouska, you must not allow what happened to stop you from doing your work. SoHMAA is important, you are important to SoHMAA." That was all she said as she used the end of her sari to dry my eyes.

"One final thing I must say to you. You know that the Indian thirst for revenge is never dead, you must always be careful. I don't think the Mehta family would try to do you harm here in America, but one never knows . . . ."

From that day onward, Dr. Alam was Dr. Alam in public and I was Dr. Mehta, but when we met and had tea, we were sisters; she was Jashina and I was Anouska.

XXX    XXX

It was not too long afterward that I began to take serious notice of something about Jashina, about Dr. Alam. She didn't seem to have a "significant other" in her life. She was a very attractive, beige/wheat colored Indian woman who wore her sari or a skirt and blouse with equal elegance. I noticed that she was never able to make her way across the campus without having one of the male students or instructors attach themselves to her. She was always friendly but she had a way about her, a way of saying, without putting it into words – "awright, that's far enough, cool it."

I invited her to have tea in my office, to discuss something. I had discovered that she was "down front," as the younger students used to say.

"Jashina, it would be impossible to notice that you're not dating anyone."

"No, I'm not," she replied and took a sip of her tea, a bit of a twinkle in her eyes.

She laughed. "Anouska, you're shameless, you know that?"

I returned her laugh. "No, just curious."

She settled her tea cup on the tray in front of her and looked very serious.

"I think, because you are an Indian, this might be easier for you to understand than if you were something else. In the Indian tradition I am Brahmacharini. Yes, I took a vow to be celibate when I was about ten years old because I wanted to devote all of my energy, all of my strength, my whole life to the study and practice of Ayuvedic medicine."

I simply stared at her. I didn't know what to say.

"Some would say that Brahmacharya is not necessary for Ayurveda, and they may be right. All I can say is that I feel that I must do the right thing for me."

We sipped a little more tea, chatted about this and that, made a date to go to a sitar concert the following week and that was that.

XXX    XXX

# CHAPTER 16

I PRAYED VERY HARD FOR a week after our tea/chat. I had never thought of myself as being very religious, but I did have strong convictions about a number of things. First off, I wanted to be the best Director SoHMAA ever had. Shamelessly, I said to myself, I want to set the bar so high that whoever follows me will have to jump very, very high, indeed.

Secondly, I felt a strange urge to cleanse my family's honor, to make them feel that they had done a good thing to help me escape from daughter-in-law servitude. Thank you, Father.

Finally, I could honestly say, prior to my marriage to Zubin, I had never experienced those sexual yearnings that writers write about, that many people spend their whole lives trying to feel. And after Zubin's death I felt no left over passion or physical needs. I felt just fine with myself. If I had a passion I could clearly identify, it was love for my work.

XXX     XXX

Jashina and I enjoyed the sitar concert immensely. The audience was about three fourths Indian and that felt good to be with our own people. We were strolling through the long corridors of UCLA when I decided to reveal myself to my sister, my friend

"Jashina, I've decided to become Brahmacharya."

She stopped, grabbed me gently by my shoulders . . . .

"I have only one question for you, are you sure you want to go this way?"

"Yes, I want to go this way to honor my father's memory."

She linked her arm thru mine as we made our way to the parking lot.

"May God bless you, Anouska."

## XXX     XXX

I can't say that a great deal changed in my life after I decided to live a celibate life. Well, maybe I should correct that statement. It became quite obvious that some people at SoHMAA assured that Dr. Alam, Jashina and I had become partners, that we were lesbian lovers. That wasn't true, but we didn't spend any time attempting to correct mistaken assumptions.

## XXX     XXX

Of course there were Gay people in our student body and on our staff, and here's how two of our Gay students inspired me to create a successful Women's Forum. Let me quickly add that all were welcome to our meetings, but I made it clear that the central focus was going to be on women's concerns/issues.

Here's the way it came about; one afternoon I was dashing from one place on campus to another place, as usual, when I saw these two young women walking toward me. They didn't take notice of me, they were talking and looking at each other. It was love, no other explanation needed.

An African-American woman with a very handsome dark face, very graceful. A dancer for sure. And an African woman who resembled Lupita N' Longó. Hard to figure out how I could make the distinction between African-American and African, but there was just something about the way they walked, the way they carried themselves that created the distinction for me.

They wore back packs and they were holding hands, very athletic looking women. I stopped them to introduce myself, something I usually did when I ran into students I didn't know. It was the best way to become acquainted with the 1,100 students on the SoHMAA campus. They disconnected hands, in a guilty kind of way, the minute I spoke to them. Uhhh ohhh . . . .

"My name is Anouska Mehta, I'm the Director of SoHMAA."

They seemed slightly ill at ease. Was it because of the hand holding? Or were they just shy? They looked to be a bit more mature looking than our usual eighteen-twenty year olds.

Gorgeous women up close.

"I'm Jewel P. Williams, my friends call me 'J.P.'"

"What's the P. for?"

"The P is for Pearl." The African-American.

"And I am Acanit P. Bigombe. I'm from Uganda and the P. in my name is also for Pearl." The African.

We shook hands, smiled at each other. The idea popped in my head like a light going on, the catalyst was the way they had "disengaged" when I stopped to speak to them. Why should they think that I would disapprove of two women holding hands?

"J.P., may I call you J.P.?"

"Of course."

"Acanit?"

"Yes, Acanit . . . ."

"Interesting name, what does it mean?"

She smiled shyly and stared at the ground for a moment.

"It means 'hard times.'"

"And you are both Pearls. I want to invite you to our Women's Forum this Saturday morning at 10 a.m. in the Living Arts building, room 200. It will be our first meeting. Think you can make it? We'll be addressing issues that mostly concern women, but we have an open door policy."

Maybe it was my imagination, but I thought I saw their eyes light up at the invitation.

"We will be there – we will be there."

"Good! Look forward to seeing you Saturday morning."

We shook hands again and I continued on my busy way. Where was I going? Oh yes, to be a part of a panel that was checking out a student complaint of sexual assault.

Now, in addition to that, I would have to write a brief mission statement about the Women's Forum, and have flyers printed and distributed about the Forum, a sudden bee that landed in my busy bonnet.

Now I would have to make certain that room 200 would be available at 10 am on Saturday. I slowed my walk to the pane/meeting. The Women's Forum was off the top of my head, but I could see the need, and how it would benefit all of the students at SoHMAA. Jashina and all the other faculty members I spoke to were enthusiastic about the idea.

"A Women's Forum? Great idea!"

XXX     XXX

I have to confess that I wasn't really prepared to see a hundred plus women show up. Room 200 was one of our tiered class rooms and it looked like women were stacked to the ceiling. There were also a few men.

I had made a snap decision not to have a set agenda, I just wanted to see how things would flow. A sentence in the mission statement – "Come, talk about yourself, what's buggin' you" — spoke to the idea I had in mind. J.P. and Acanit were there, third row, center. By way of explaining what I thought this Forum should be about, I made two strong recommendations.

"We don't want to talk about shallow stuff, and we will not argue needlessly. Now, who's first?"

I could practically feel some people draw into their shells.

"I will be first." Acanit made a graceful stroll to the front of the class and stood there for a beat. She had great natural stage presence.

"My name is Acanit Pearl Bigombe. I come from the country of Uganda. I(am now twenty-three years old; before I was twelve I had been raped six times by the men in our village. They said that was the best way for them to make a woman out of me. They saw that I was gay and they wanted to kill this urge, this demon in me. This what they saw.

I don't really think they were trying to do anything but enjoy themselves with my body."

It seemed that a cloud had drifted across the sun, making the room look dim for a few minutes. I saw a few women crying quietly. Well, I had recommend that we should avoid the shallow stuff, but I had no idea it would get this deep so soon.

"As many of you may already know, the homophobia that exists in Uganda was promoted and, I should say, paid for by so called Evangelists from the United States. I cannot say I understand why these rich, white, so called Evangelists decided to bring this bigotry, their intolerant attitudes, their arrogance to my poor little county.

But they did, and many people have been hurt and even killed by those who feel that they have a God given right to tell us who we should love."

J.P. and Acanit exchanged tender, coded looks.

"I don't have a prepared speech and, I must confess, I'm talking to you from the heart. This is the first time that I have spoken openly, other than to my partner, sitting just there. I have not had the opportunity to speak to so many at the same time, so I am a little nervous."

Michelle Roland, one of our best students spoke quietly, but firmly.

"Don't be nervous, sister, we're with you."

Acanit gave Michelle a grateful smile.

"What I must ask of you to do for me, for the poor people in Uganda, is to shine a light on the situation that exists there. Things are slightly better than they used to be, but there is still a huge undercurrent of hatred for LGBT people. There are still terrible penalties in place for those of us who are not what others want us to be."

"What can we do?" Someone asked from the upper tier.

"There are many, many things. I will ask for only four; please fax, e-mail, Facebook, anything to your elected officials, to tell them to shutdown al aid to Uganda until the government treats its LGBT community with respect. The money drought will have a great effect. Yes, some poor, deserving people will suffer, but the society as a whole will benefit.

Number two, fax, e-mail, communicate with the people of Uganda. One of the things I've found out about people to people contact is that we have more in common than we think. We simply have to get to know each other.

Number three, go to Uganda if you can, it's a beautiful country and your presence would make it even more so.

Finally, bring Uganda onto your screens, into your lives; I'm sorry, I know I'm being redundant but I can't think of anything else to say. Thank you very much . . . ."

There was a soft pattering of hands, no grand ovation, or shouts of approval, just a soft, serious pattering of hands.

J.P. gave her partner a quick peck on her cheek as she strolled to the front of the room, to take her place.

"My name is Jewel Pearl Williams and I am very pleased and proud to join you this morning. Acanit, my partner, just gave you a glimpse of what life was like for her in Uganda, as a Gay woman, I had experiences similar to hers, as an openly Gay woman in 'the great state of Miss'ssippi,'

I had the very bad luck to be born into a family of ol' fashioned, rock-hide-bound Baptist Fundamentalists. My Grandfather was a preacher, my father is a preacher, my brother Thomas is going to be a preacher. Growing up I was surrounded by this rock-hide religiosity.

Like Acanit, I was raped several times by men who professed to being 'Christians.' Like they said to her; "we're doing this to make you a woman.' I went to the police, we had a force of four white policemen in the small town of Chitlin' Switch. Four white cops were not in our community to 'protect and serve,' but to oppress and humiliate.

When I went to the police station to file a complaint about the first rape, the desk sergeant laughed in my face.

'Who the hell wants to rape you?'

"It's already been done, that's why I'm reporting his crime to you." I was about fifteen at the time.

The police treated me like I was the criminal.

"Now, tell us the truth, just what did you do to cause this boy to wanna get inside your underwear?"

"I didn't do anything and 'the boy' I'm asking to be arrested is a forty-three-year-old man."

The second time this happened, about three months later, when two men, two strong Black men, pulled me into a van one night and did what they wanted to do 'til dawn, then they kicked me out in an alley.

My father didn't want to hear my story, and when he heard it he didn't believe it.

"I'll teach ya to stay out all night and come up in heah lyin' to me!"

He pulled his razor strop down from the bathroom wall and whipped me real hard. I still have welts from that first razor stroppin'."

I saw women nodding in agreement with "J.P.'s" story. Evidently, they knew something about parental abuse too. My blessed father had only spoken to me – "Anouska, dear."

"I was whipped regularly after that, for any reason whatsoever. I was whipped hardest for not wanting to go to church. Who wants to go stare her rapists in the face every Sunday?"

It was the first meeting of our Women's Forum and I will never forget it. "J.P." was an incredible spokesperson for the freedom we all need to explore in our inner selves.

"I was seventeen and I had had enough, I decided to split the scene."

The students gave a hip laugh and a murmur of appreciation for her decision "to split the scene."

"I wound up in San Francisco. Yeahhh, the wild beast city. I spent exactly six months smokin' the smoke, tootin' the blow, droppin' all the acid I could find. But there came a moment, when the bong was being passed to me for the fifth time, that a bell rang off in my head that said, "hey girl, you didn't run away from the Chitlin Switch scene just to smoke, toot, drop and nut off."

I got involved with this African-American organization that was trying to establish schools for girls, especially in Kenya, Burundi, Uganda. No one wanted to tackle Uganda. I thought I was tough enough to tackle anything after all of the razor stop whippings I had survived. Almost as an afterthought, one of the organization's leaders approached me.

"Uhh, sister J.P., you do know that there is a very <u>strong</u> anti-Gay sentiment in Uganda right now?"

"I didn't know, but now that you've told me, so what should I do? Should I deny who I am in order to help my brothers 'n sisters?"

"J.P." was a seasoned speaker who shied away from preaching, she simply laid it out.

"I have to tell you, straight up, I was ready to pull up my tent pegs and retreat back to the land of milk 'n money, America. I was teaching English in a small village near Kampala, the capital, when I met Acanit. My stated aim in this place was to help these girls, these sisters, learn how to read and write proper English.

I knew, first hand, coming from America, that the right use of language could mean a better income, a brighter future. Think about it, some honest, ex-colonial white folks had figured it out; if we can keep these ex-colonials within our grip by using our language we'll always have them by the short hairs."

A few people smothered their laughter.

"And there I was, teaching the master's language. I felt very ambivalent about my job. And then Acanit came into my classroom, into my heart. It only took a few days, 'specially after I heard her horror story, that I decided that we had to get out of Uganda. Ever had the feeling that the walls were closing in on you?

That's the feeling we had. Truth be told, the walls <u>were</u> closing in on us. The walls of a prison cell. We got out just a day or so before I was going to be arrested. No telling what they were going to do to Acanit. We got

155

out – with help from a number of courageous Ugandans. 'Mr. Fixit', for example, who helped Acanit get the proper papers. And didn't charge us an arm and leg either.

We had decided that our best chance to get out of Africa would be for us to get to the west coast, to Ghana, where my organization had connections. It took us six month, traveling thru war zones in Zaire, the Congo, places that bordered on chaos, anarchy, craziness, for us to reach Accra, Ghana, West Africa.

But, as you can see, to make a long story short, we made it."

The audience erupted in spontaneous applause. "J.P.", bowed slightly and returned to sit beside her partner. They came in a slow, almost choreographed succession after her.

"Lady Saudi;" "I was seven years old when my mother, my two aunts and one of our neighbors suddenly grabbed me and took me into a room and spread legged me on a table. I couldn't figure out what was happening.

And then this woman with a sharp razor came into the room, mumbled a few words and proceeded to cut on my private parts. The "operation" that she performed is called a clitorectomy. I felt that I was going to die from the pain. I think that this one horrible thing is responsible for me wanting to become a doctor, someone who could prevent others from ever feeling the pain I once experienced."

There were several of those terrible stories, which were lightened, thank God, by other stories.

"We had a chance to travel across this great, beautiful country, from the cold and snow of the east, to the sun and warmth of the west. I have to admit, I love both sides, the contrasts . . . ."

Mr. K., "I will simply call myself 'Mr. K.' because I might still have enemies around, people who would kill me for saying that I am very glad to be an American citizen now. Being an American means that I am now one of the warm, wonderful people who make America what it is.

I recognize that everything is not absolutely honky dorey here, but I have to say that I see evidence that the people, the politicians, whoever, are making an effort to solve the problems, they are not allowed to fester like open wounds. I know every day that I live in this glorious land, that I can have the audacity to be free, to be optimistic, to have hope."

After two sold hours of the bitter and the sweet, I was given the job of folding the tent because room 200 was going to be used for a class in herbal recognition and use. SoHMAA was a busy place.

What could I say that hadn't been said, how could I wrap this up and prepare curious minds for the next Saturday, the next meeting of the Women's Forum? I took a deep breath and gave my feelings free play, the way several of our speakers had done.

"While I was listening to what we just heard, I wasn't thinking about what I could say at the end of this because I think it is just the beginning."

I was a bit startled by erupting applause. I took another deep breath.

"I would like to suggest to those who have shared some of their terrible memories with us, those who have suffered incredible hardship and pain; I would like to suggest that you think of yourselves as clams."

I had to smile at the puzzled expressions that greeted my novel suggestion.

"I'm not saying – become clams, I'm saying, think of yourselves as human clams who've had horrible irritants penetrate your shells. So, in Nature, what does the clam do when the irritant finds its way into the clam's insides? It fights back by secreting a milky substance that coats the irritant, neutralizes it.

It can take a long time for this secretion to happen, for the irritation to be fully coated, but as we know, the final result can often be a beautiful pearl. Or two beautiful pearls, like 'J.P.' and Acanit."

The applause come in waves and I felt enveloped by the warmth. Later, as Jashina and I went for chai at the Student Center, she sat across from me and whispered . . . .

"I call it the 'Sermon of the Pearls,' I think you should tell it as often as possible."

XXX     XXX

# CHAPTER 17

CoCo Chen-Lane and Verona Obregon-Hoover stacked the pages they had just read into two neat piles, CoCo with the original, Verona with the copy. They stared across the copy desk in the basement of their Kosmic Muffin Publishing House.

"Coco, we have to publish this."

"I knew you would say that."

"I have to admit, I didn't have high hopes about the manuscript after we received Dr. Metha's query letter. All I could think was – uhh – ohh – we're getting ready to receive a big dose of academic diarrhea."

"I'll second that, in addition I was up a tree about what we were going to say to Dan and Jonathan about rejecting their mentor's work."

"Well, thank God, we've been spared the pain of making the second rejection in Kosmic Muffin's history.

XXX      XXX

"Dan, did CoCo tell you that they've received a manuscript from Dr. Mehta?"

"Yeah, she told me but she won't let me read it. How about you?"

"Same here, Verona simply says – "It's very good, we think it'll make a very good read when it's released."

"I had no idea Dr. Mehta was a writer."

"I'm sure she must've thought the same thing about us before 'Ancestral Meridians' hit the top of the Book Review chart."

XXX      XXX

Two years after Dr. Mehta's book, 'Pearls' was released, Kosmic Muffin Publishing House was given serious shout outs and a $5,000.00 award for being one of the best small, independent publishing houses in the country.

"CoCo, you know something" I've been thinking seriously about giving up my day job."

"I've given that a little thought too. The problem is that I get so much satisfaction from doing what I do in the mental health field, it's like a double dip of something you like."

"I wish I could say the same but, as you know, the so called justice system is not very just and not such a good system either."

Six months later, Dr. Dan Lane II, Dr. Jonathan Hoover and Dr. Mehta sat on a dais in the Fine Arts Auditorium (Pasadena, California) to receive $1,500.00 checks and literary plaque awards, praising Dr. Daniel Lane II and Dr. Jonathan Hoover for their books, "Ancestral Meridians" and "Internal Discussions." Dr. Mehta also received a $2,500.00 check and a literary award, praising her honesty, her excellent writing, and the promise "she shows as a beginning writer."

During the course of the ceremony, Verona leaned over to whisper to CoCo; "CoCo, I've decided to give up my day job."

"When did you decide to do that?"

"Last night, when Jonathan was reading the first three chapters of the new book he and Dan just finished . . . ."

"No wonder my husband has had this spacey look in his eyes for the past few months."

"Have you read it?"

"Haven't had time, what's the title and what's it about?"

"They call it 'Spiritual Intersections, Eshu Meridians'."

"And who, may I ask, is Eshu?"

"I think he's supposed to be the Lord of the Crossroads in Yoruba mythology, something like that."

"These guys are getting more and more out of the box, the older they get."

"You got that right, girlfriend, you got that right."

XXX      XXX

159

Dr. Daniel Lane II, his wife CoCo, and Dr. Jonathan Hoover and his wife, Verona, slowly made their way around the ballroom, being greeted, stopped for selfies, praised, chatted up by single people, duos, trios, clusters of people, colleagues, friends, ex-patients. They held their glasses of excellent white wine at port arms, completely enjoying the vibes, tripping on the sight and sounds of people that they hadn't seen in years.

"If Robert 'Mr. Egypt' shows up I'm runnin' out of here," Jonathan whispered into his friends' ear.

"We'll be right behind you . . . ."

## XXX    XXX

The invitation to dedicate an evening to Dr. Daniel Lane II and Dr. Jonathan Hoover was the brainchild of Danilov Petrovich, one of the patients they had treated jointly, as young interns.

"You are invited to share an evening with two men who have spent their working lives helping other people, using their herbal knowledge, their expert acupuncture, their chiropractical expertise. Join us . . . . Dinner (Vegan, etc.) will be served at 6 pm; good vibes, corny jokes and warm fellowship will prevail,

Sincerely yours,
Danilov Petrovich and Friends."

That was all it took for the ballroom to be filled (capacity 850) with more than a thousand people. There were no fire marshals in the house. There were friends who simply exchanged a coded wink and an upheld glass in the direction of the honorees, duos who insisted on receiving autographs – "We want to remember that you all pinned us."

It became quite warm and quite fuzzy, what with all the people present, who all had resurgent memories – "Hey, 'til Dr. Hoover got to me, I thought that my neck was always supposed to feel like a whiplash."

"It was my left leg, draggin' the bad boy behind me like a piece of extra luggage. Dr. Lane sliced off the excess fat."

"I'm sure that Dr. Hoover doesn't want to talk about his, but my semi-spent libido got a real shot in the . . . uhh, 'arm' from his acupuncture."

The scene was buzzed from people exchanging experiences with the men being honored. It was all pre-"dinner now being served" because it seemed like an avenue suddenly opened up between the doctors and Dr. Mehta. The people in the ballroom applauded. Dr. Mehta's smile pulled Daniel and Jonathan into her arms.

"You two are like the sons I never had," she whispered as they shared a three-way embrace. The applause grew louder, a spontaneous gesture of pleasure to see the mentor and her students together again.

The avenue opened in the direction of the dining room. Dr. Mehta glanced at her wristwatch, it was ten to six. She was pleased to see that the event was taking place on time. Of course there would be remarks from the elevated dais, but what else could one do if you placed them on elevated pedestals?

"I heard the news of your invitation (she exchanged glances with both of them) this morning. Are you going?"

Daniel answered for both of them. "Dr. Mehta, when our President calls, I, we feel obligated to go."

"What seems to be her problem?"

"From the non-classified document she sent us, it seems that she might have a bit or arthritis, or perhaps sciatica. I can't imagine what the effect would be, of dragging yourself up in down events at campaign rallies, etc. I think we expect too much out of politicians who are not seasoned athletes. Obama tried to set the tone but they ignored him. But he's gone now and we're in a different game."

"We'll be able to determine what's wrong with the President when we get to the White House, and we will be able to deal with her problems. That's why she called on SoHMAA, on us."

"Daniel, Jonathan, as you both know this is the first time we have had a female president, and the first time physicians from SoHMAA have been invited to treat our president – so, do your best, make SoHMAA proud."

"Yes M'am . . . ."

"Yes M'am . . . ."

"Dinner is now being served . . . ."

XXX    XXX

# EPILOGUE

"I THINK ONE OF THE things that impressed me most was her cool, her way of dealing with emergencies, crisis situations,,,,"

"Yeah, that was something to see, how many emergencies did she have to deal with during our three days with her?"

"Dan, to be honest, I lost count. I had a vague idea of what it was like to be the President, but she demonstrated what it was <u>really</u> like to be the President – a crisis every hour, with semi-crisises stuff in between."

They allowed a thoughtful minute to interrupt their random dialogue as they watched a bold Autumn sun slowly slip behind the glistening blue-green waters of the Pacific, stretching thousands of miles in front of them. Autumn on Signal Hill, in Long Beach, California, two doctors exchanging free form confidential observations.

Who else could they talk to? They had sworn to be silent, not to discuss what they had done with the President of the United States over the course of a three-day treatment session.

"You know the first time I felt the tension in her shoulders, it felt like I was dealing with coils of rope."

"Dan, you've just identified one of the things I love about the Chiro element of SoHMAA therapy, if we can call it that?"

Dan made a theatrical moment of looking over both shoulders, as though he was searching for someone who might be eavesdropping on them.

"O.k., all clear, no one around to rat us out, call it what you like." They exchanged smiles, enjoying each others humor.

"Good. What I like about the chiropractical element is that you can often feel, see immediate results. Acupuncture? Well, we know you don't always get immediate results."

"Ordinarily I would agree with you, but I do think our use of the Golden Needles definitely saved that woman's life."

"I don't doubt that for a minute. I had some idea of what could happen to a person when they were subjected to mind boggling lies, vicious attacks on their ideas, their character, the way they look, their religious beliefs even, but I've never had the opportunity to treat someone who had dealt with all of that – who had dealt with politics at the sewerage level."

"Jonathan, my friend, one must remember that American politics have always been a bit rough around the edges."

"Nothing to argue about there. But I think this last general election should open the door for extreme vetting, **Extreme** vetting for would be politicians who have mental health issues."

"You're not talking about the President?"

"No, no, I'm not talking about the President, I'm talking about the guy who ran against the President, who had so many transparent mental health issues that many members of his own party, colloquially called, 'The White guys' Party,' ran away from him."

"Yeah, poor White folks. I have to admit I feel a bit for them, 'specially the ones who thought that an egomaniacal, pathological liar was going to make them the rulers of America again."

"Sad . . . ."

Twilight exercisers, people who had avoided the bright sun of an Autumn day, suddenly seemed to surge around them. The doctors measured the exercisers with expert perceptions.

"O my God! Why would a woman that skinny be running up and down this hill?"

"It's called anorexia, Dr. Lane, sheer anorexia."

"And look at those people over there, doing all of those incredibly bad things to their bodies. What the hell are they doing?"

"They call it, 'Loosening up.' Or sometimes, 'Limbering up.' You're familiar with these negative, body damaging exercise, are you not?"

Once again they allowed themselves the space to reflect on random thoughts for a few moments.

"You think Master Tam was the right Tai Chi teacher for the President?"

"Dan, read my lips – we couldn't've made a better choice. I can't think of any Tai Chi Master in this country better suited to teach the President of the United States Tai Chi."

"Gotta agree with you. You know she's flying him in twice a month for classes."

"That's great, that's what she needed, someone who could help her relieve stress, help with the flexibility stuff, do all of the things that Tai Chi can do."

"I wonder how it's going with them?"

XXX    XXX

"Last time, Lady President, you do good. Today you do no good. No problem, we fix. Sometimes <u>I</u> do good, sometimes <u>I</u> do no good. No matter. When you do this one you think too much. You don't think too much. You do better.

We don't talk talk talk. We do this one, this way, Needle at the bottom of the sea. Now relax, do this one, no hurry. You United States of America? You not perfect. Stop. You don't know. Think Nothing. Keep do it. You give one you get one. You try to do good, you do no good. Breathe in, breathe out. You *unnerstand* my meaning? Nobody perfect. Not wrong, but ugly. Better. Do it and you think how you feel? Nobody can show you. You believe yourself. You up yourself. But still no good. Like Meditation. Difficult, but I sure you can get it."

XXX    XXX

"What time are we meeting Coco and Verona at Ichiban?"

"7:30. But let's make ourselves ten minutes late."

"Why?"

"Just because we're sipping the twilight a little longer, my friend, just because we're . . . ."

"Sipping the twilight a little longer." I hope we're not drunk when we get there."

"No problem, they'll understand. They've always understood. Remember, they were the ones who formed the Kosmic Muffin Publishing House to publish 'Ancestral Meridians'."

165

"I'll never forget it."

XXX    XXX

*"A tenth planet has been discovered, all of the details have not been revealed about how much is known, or unknown about this planet, other than the fact that it is ten times larger than Earth. It has been tentatively named #10 and that's it for the moment. Stay tuned."*

# POSTSCRIPT

*On November 8th, 2016, the outmoded Electoral College enabled the unimaginable to happen; therefore, I could not include that event in this work of fiction.*

*"'Alternative facts' are often stranger than fiction"*

*– Zola Salena-Hawkins*

# RESEARCH REFERENCES

1. http://www.saghaei.net/Kbase/acupuncture_technique/principles/
   needling/sedating_and_tonifying.html_
2. Acupuncture A Scientific Appraisal by E. Ernst and A. White
3. rheumatology.oxfordjournals.org.content/43/5/662.Full
   A brief history of acupuncture by A. White and E. Ernst.
4. www. ancient-egypt-online.come/daily-life-in-ancient-egypt.html.
5. www.Sptimes.com/Egypt/EgyptCredit4.2html
6. www.wikihow.com/Divorce-a-Missing-Spouse-in-the-USA
7. www.pbs.org/black-culture/shows/list/underground-railroad/
   stories-freedom/henry-box-brown/Freedom Marker: Courage and
   Creativity by Dr. Bryan Walls
8. "Henry Box Brown" -- Radio Play by Odie Hawkins, Sears Radio
   Theater, aired April 30, 1979 – Episode #61
9. http://www.ncbi.nlm.nih.gov/pmc/articles/PMC3312187/

Sex Reassignment Surgery in the Female-to-Male Transsexual
Stan J. Monstrey, M.D., Ph.D.; Peter Ceulemans, M.D.; Piet Hoebeki,
M.D., Ph.D.

Printed in the United States
By Bookmasters